Came to Stay

Maria Giuliani

Last night I dreamed that I came face to face with a picture I had done and forgotten, a forest done in simple movement, just forms of trees moving in space. That is the third time I have seen pictures in my dreams, a glint of what I am striving to attain.

— Emily Carr

PROLOGUE

I ran into someone from high school today—Janie Palmer, the school sweetheart. She was the girl that everybody liked... I always envied her that. I mean, it's not that I had issues or anything, I just always felt I had to work harder for everything than she did. That was probably just my perception as an angst-filled teenager, lacking in confidence. For me, confidence was learned over time and with experience, it was something I grew into rather than something naturally occurring. Particularly when it came to social relationships.

Janie is married now—of course she is. Sigh. I don't really care, honestly. But I spoke with Ma afterwards and she pulled out her guilt card—going on and on about the grandkids she'll never have—and admittedly, it put me in a funk.

Anyway, Janie seems to have grown into a perfectly lovely adult with a perfectly lovely life. She's been married for twelve years and has four kids. Four! All between the ages of two and ten. So perfectly aligned. She seemed happy with her life. Tired, granted. But happy. She said that being a mother was her chosen career—I never thought of it like that. Actually, that's not true. That is exactly how I thought of motherhood. Which is exactly why I'm not a mom. But hearing her say those words, so clearly and without reservation, it struck a nerve.

When she asked me about my life and my career—something that I am proud of, something that I do feel confident about—my responses felt hollow. She was genuinely interested in the work that I do, and she never once gave me "Aww, you're all alone" eyes, but still, for the first time in...ever...I felt like it wasn't enough. It didn't help that her youngest kid was asleep in the stroller and making incredibly adorable sleep faces.

It's fine. I've made my choices in life and I don't have any regrets. And I know without a doubt that I am okay. But, if I'm allowed a 'but,' I suppose it's only human to question.

CHAPTER ONE

For her there was nothing quite as sensual as the feel of a brush gliding through globs of paint. The sensation consumed her, all her concentration, all her being—she was without thought, operating purely on feeling and instinct. The brush gliding across the canvas—sometimes swooshing, sometimes moving with excruciating slowness, but always with intention —was merely an extension of her experienced hand. She knew this brush, she knew paint, she knew this world.

Chiara had spent the past twenty years building her career as an artist, working her way up through Montreal's many galleries, from one room shows to personalized exposés, to finally having her art displayed on some of the city's more prominent contemporary art stages. She worked hard at her art, was dedicated to it, and the art community widely respected her dedication. To them, she was the real deal.

Introverted, spiritual and free-spirited, she was also practical, down to earth and focused when it came to getting things done, particularly when it came to her work. Chiara was a project-oriented person. Once an idea impregnated itself in her mind, she would go all in, cultivating it, growing it, breathing it until the point where she determined, by some intrinsic sense of accomplishment, that the artwork was complete. In between projects she allowed herself to dream, freely, finding this the surest way of attracting inspiration.

"You are a true artist," Paul said, in tune with the moment at hand as always.

Chiara had been leaning as far forward on her stool as her balance would allow, her face a mere inch from the canvas as she worked. Her dark brown hair was down around her shoulders, the loose curls springing forward around her cheeks, precariously in danger of being painted themselves.

She allowed a small smirk to crack through her concentration. "And you, sir, had better just spit it out."

Chiara, as current artist-in-residence at *Les Galeries Bleues,* was spending her Sunday afternoon painting publicly in one of the gallery spaces, open to gazing and questioning from any who passed by. She was happy to discuss her work with anyone who truly wondered, yet she always found these events rather tiring. It was hard for her to divide her attention between creation and explanation—and crowds, in general, just exhausted her. She was always happier when left alone with her paints and brushes.

Paul, the gallery manager and one of her closest friends of the past decade, had come in to check on her. Knowing her as well as he did, he knew she'd been off the past few weeks, not herself, and he was hoping to get a glimpse into what was on her mind.

Paul was a stout man, his round face defined by a thick and sculpted beard. Behind his square glasses were soft hazel eyes. By his overall jovial appearance, he was an instantly likeable character, but anyone who spent even ten minutes with him would know that he also possessed a sharp wit and admirable intelligence. It was his wit that first brought he and Chiara together as friends, and on this level that their friendship was steadfastly grounded.

"Spit what out, exactly?" And then, without waiting for an answer, "It's just that, brilliant as you are with a paintbrush, you suck at real life. There's something bothering you, you can't really explain it, and because you can't, you won't even talk about it. You're dumb."

At that she laughed. "Gee, thanks."

He smiled mischievously. "No, but seriously. Talk to me."

"I don't know, honestly. I mean…" With a large sigh, she continued. "My birthday is in a few weeks. I think that has something to do with it."

"Ah, the proverbial mid-life crisis, is it? You're turning forty so everything in your life is under the microscope? As long as you don't give up painting," he warned. "So, what are you thinking? Time for a Vespa? A new 'do? What if you bleached your hair blond, would that be drastic enough?"

"Don't you ever stop?" she laughed again. There was a reason she kept Paul around.

"Tell me then but, be honest."

"It's just... When I was nineteen, my neighbour got pregnant. She was young, mid-twenties, had gone to university for something or other, and then got married and pregnant and never went back to the career she studied for. It was like, whatever she had planned for her life went out the window for a husband and kids. And I remember thinking that that was it. Either you married and had kids, and then, when the kids are old enough, figure out your life, or, dedicate yourself to your career from the outset and wait on the husband and kids. In my nineteen-year-old mind, I decided that you couldn't grow both a career and a family at the same time, that you needed to choose which one to prioritize first. I knew what I wanted to be in life, I've always known, and I didn't want to jeopardize that. So, I made my choice. I chose art. I chose my passion. But, —and this is a big 'but'—I always figured the rest would follow, you know? Once I was established, once my career took on a life of its own. But it never did. Now I'm staring forty in the face and I have all these…questions? Doubts?"

She grew silent then, contemplative. Sad. Paul could feel the sadness sinking into her bones. Looking around and noticing the empty gallery, he took the paintbrush from her hand, placed it down on the pallet, and gave her one of his famous bear hugs. Holding her until he felt the sadness dissipate a little, he spoke to her as he let go.

"Listen to me. You've done great, kid. You did everything right. You built the career of your dreams and no one could be prouder. Take a break. You need a break. Clear your head, go celebrate your birth, get away from all this for a while. Trust me. A change of pace will help you clear your mind. All will feel right in the world with time, I promise."

She gave Paul an appreciative smile. She saw the truth in what he was saying and valued this bit of perspective. It had been ages since her last vacation, the back of her neck began to tingle at the mere thought of beach and ocean.

They were interrupted then by a group of university-aged friends who were bee-lining directly for Chiara. They were obviously students, spending their Sunday afternoon on an elective field trip. Paul gave her arm a soft squeeze as she took a deep breath and picked up her brush. She was a professional first.

"I'll leave you to it but, do me a favour. Before you go, there's a notice up by the staff exit that I just put up today. It's from an old acquaintance of mine. Could be interesting." He turned then as the students swarmed in, leaving her to do what she did best.

Later, after the gallery goers had thinned out and her station had been cleared, after she'd had just about all the peopling she could handle for one day, she signed out of the security log and paused, intentionally, in front of the notice board while she gathered her belongings. She allowed her eyes to slowly move their way across the board as she put on a light jacket, then stopped suddenly, only one sleeve on, as she came upon the homemade flyer that Paul must have been referring to. He knew. He always knew. Tearing off a small slip bearing a phone number and email address, she left for home.

———————

Chiara's condo was the ground level of a typical Montreal triplex. It was what was generally referred to as a five and a half, a residence consisting of five rooms and a bathroom. Aside from the large eat-in kitchen and spacious living room, there were three bedrooms—a lot of space for someone single, yet very useful to Chiara. Aside from her own bedroom, which was the second largest of the rooms, Chiara used the smallest bedroom as her home office and guest room and reserved the largest room for her personal home studio. Years earlier, she had considered the possibility of renting a studio separate from her home environment, but when it came down to it, she appreciated being able to paint late into the night, or early in the wee hours of the day if the occasion called for it, without having to waste time in transit. As such, virtually all her pajamas had paint on them, but this was a sacrifice she was willing to concede for the freedom to remain home.

Returning home that evening, she headed immediately toward her tiny backyard. Walking its small perimeter, she glanced at the perennials just starting to peek green through soil. Herbs of mint and oregano, creeping thyme, and a large sage bush made up most of the small garden. As she walked, she envisioned where she might plant flowers to add some colour to the yard, thinking in shades of red and purple against the backdrop of a rather drab grey fence. Beyond the fence the sounds of the city played a continuous soundtrack to Chiara's daily life, its hum often forgotten yet always conspicuously present.

Normally, by the start of May, Chiara would feel open, energetic and excited by the freshness of the spring air and official retiring of her winter layers. She was normally not immune to the sense of rejuvenation that came with spring, the vibration amplified by it being her birth month. This May, however, brought no such excitement, and on this night in particular, Chiara left her garden emotionally untouched by its promise of lush greenery and earthy scents.

Returning indoors she poured herself a glass of merlot, carrying it with her to her bedroom where she changed into her most comfortable pajamas. Grabbing her laptop from the edge of the bed, where she'd dropped it that morning, she continued on into the living room, plopping herself down in her favourite spot at the end of the sofa.

This had become her nightly routine. A glass of wine on the end table beside her, feet rested up on the tufted ottoman, television turned on to any program she could shut her mind to. Looking around the room it dawned on her, for the second time that day, that Paul had been right. She was in a rut, she needed change.

Suddenly motivated, she retrieved the slip of paper she had torn from the notice board that afternoon. Opening her laptop, she began to type.

———————————

"The tests have come back, Giovanni—"

"Cancer? Just tell me the truth, Doctor."

Dr. Bloomberg pursed his lips, gently. He had had this conversation more times than he wished to count over the course of his lengthy medical career, and it never got easier. But patients like Giovanni, those who found strength in the face of death, who chose to be a rock for the loved ones they were leaving behind, had the opposite effect on the doctor, tending to make it more difficult for him to maintain an air of self-assuredness. He was an emotional man, despite the rigid exterior it was his duty to present at times like these. It was easier for him to handle an emotional outburst than the strong stoicism of the man sitting before him. He found it unsettling, and he squirmed mildly in his seat before continuing.

Speaking to Giovanni, but looking at his wife, he confirmed the diagnosis. "Yes, it is cancer. Giovanni—the cancer started in your prostate. On its own it could have been treated, but—"

"I told him! I told you! Go to the doctor, I said it a hundred times. But did he listen? No!"

"Mrs. Costa—Giovanni, the cancer has spread to other organs. It has metastasized quite rapidly from what we can tell."

"So, what can we do? Doctor? What are the—"

"Sofia—"

Giovanni said his wife's name in a tone she knew well. He wanted her to allow the doctor to finish the diagnosis. The husband and wife turned their sights back to Dr. Bloomberg, prompting him to continue.

"It's stage four cancer, and it's spreading quickly. A few months ago, maybe I would have recommended treatment but, at this point... I don't recommend treatment at this time." He stopped there, allowing the couple time to process the truth of what he was saying. Next he would inform them about protocol, provide them with information on what physical changes to expect, and ways to keep Giovanni as comfortable as possible. There would be many questions, particularly from Mrs. Costa. But not before they asked the one question that all people in this position need to ask; the one answer that it is human nature to seek. This was the one answer Dr. Bloomberg regretted having to give.

"How much, Doctor? How much time do I have?"

"But you *have* to tell her!"

"Sofia, it's my decision. I said no!"

"Giovanni, come on. We didn't tell her about the tests because you didn't want to worry her, but this is different. You're her father, she has a right to know."

"So, we'll tell her, but not until she gets back."

"That's weeks from now! You heard the doctor, you don't have time—"

"Yes. And she deserves to enjoy this vacation before we tell her. It's her birthday, Sofia. I don't want it overshadowed by sickness and death. For the rest of her life, every time her birthday draws near, it would be a constant reminder. Let her go have some fun, let her go enjoy herself. When she comes back, then we tell her."

"She's not a child anymore. Giovanni, she's forty years old."

"I know, but I am still her father. I can protect her this one last time."

Tearing up, she turned away. She knew she could not convince him otherwise. "You stubborn, stubborn man."

CHAPTER TWO

The drive from the St. John's airport had been beautiful but long. She was tired, and still a little unsure about what she was doing. As she turned off the main highway onto a secondary road, she saw a sign for her final destination, Came to Stay, thirty-six kilometres ahead. She couldn't help but smile every time she came across that name, or any of the other cheeky town names she'd come to learn of during her limited research. Come by Chance, A Heart's Desire, Cupid's Crossing, Happy Adventure—she instinctively understood that Newfoundlanders were not ones to take themselves too seriously. "This place may just be the therapy I need after all," she said quietly to herself.

She pulled off the main road once more and was struck instantly by a view of the ocean in all its immense glory. It took her breath away, she decided to pull to the side of the road so she could step out and enjoy it. Leaning against the hood of her rental, she allowed her mind to lose itself in the beautiful vista, the sound of the crashing waves, and the thick scent of the salty air. Chiara had always been someone who felt with her whole body and in this moment, it was as though she was one with her surroundings. She was so lost in the moment that she didn't even hear the car that pulled up behind hers; so startled, when a few minutes later she heard someone speak.

"Beautiful, isn't it?"

Chiara turned with a jolt to find a man standing a car's length behind her, his hatchback parked slightly off the road with the door left wide open. She had been so immersed in her senses that it took her mind some time to catch up to this sudden snap to reality. She was agitated for being caught off guard and, slightly embarrassed for looking startled. She was close to saying something snippy as a result, but her words caught in her throat as she took in the person before her.

He was slightly taller than average, a full head taller than herself. He had strong shoulders, she could tell, and her eyes fixated on them for a few seconds too long before moving up to his face. There she found herself looking into the clearest blue eyes she had ever seen.

"It's beautiful, eh?" he tried again.

His voice was a bit gruff, a working man's voice, which matched perfectly with his working man's body. Chiara had always had an appreciation for muscles that looked like they were earned through hard work and physical labour, and not only through working out at the gym. It reminded her of her father, whom she respected more than any other person alive, and who had spent years supporting his family by working long hours in construction. Growing up, knowing her father to be a good man, she had engrained certain attributes in her mind as attributes that she assumed would define any good man. On instinct she immediately felt safe with this man before her, despite him being, still, a complete stranger.

He was standing there, still waiting for her to speak, having decided not to rush her or interrupt her thoughts any further. He was watching her though, closely, as she was looking upon him, and forming thoughts of his own.

After what could only be described as an embarrassingly long period of silence, Chiara managed to pull herself together, finding her voice just as she felt a flush move across her cheeks. "It's amazing. Truly."

"From away, are you?" he asked as he casually moved a hand through his sandy-coloured hair. Contrary to her dark Sicilian complexion, he looked as though he was born of the beach, the ocean, the sun on the waves. His hair was just long enough to form wispy wings around his face, the rest of his full head of hair showing streaks of blonde moving gently through the thick waves. His face itself was strong and angular, slightly wrinkled by time and the elements, yet possessed a boyish charm, especially when he grinned.

"I am, yes. Just arriving from Montreal."

"Just passing through?"

"Looking for my rental, actually." Happy for the opportunity for something concrete to discuss, something to minimize her awkwardness, she stepped around to the car window and grabbed the printed instructions from the dashboard. "The instructions are a little vague. I, uh, had just pulled off to get my bearings. It says to look for the house with the green roof?"

"You're renting the Boyd place, then?" It was less a question than a statement, his tone was casual and certain. Turning his direction across the road, he waved his arm in a grand gesture. She turned to look as well and noticed, for the first time, that there were really only a few houses, perhaps twenty at most, making up this little community. Each could be seen from the main road (arguably the only road, the others looking more like extended driveways than proper roads). The beach lay at the lowest point of town, the landscape moving progressively upward as it moved inland. It was a rugged landscape, rocky, its ruggedness smoothed over by spurts of trees and shrubbery, all set before a backdrop of dense greenery. It was too early in the season yet, but Chiara could imagine wildflowers springing up from the rocks and untamed grass, mentally adding natural highlights of white, purple and blue to the scene before her.

From this perspective she could see every rooftop of

every saltbox home, and immediately felt sheepish. "Not so vague after all, I suppose," she said. The houses themselves came in every colour—turquoise, crimson, lilac, buttercup and pure white—each home unique and unbridled by paint. Coming from a city with rows of homes in remarkable uniformity, she found the inclination toward colour refreshing. Looking up at the town from the beach, her fingers began to tingle, longing for a brush to hold.

The man smiled, a shy and crooked smile, and offered, "A lot of these coastal villages are all the same. Just a few houses scattered about, faces to the sea, backs to the land. Welcome to Newfoundland. Will you be needing any assistance? Or, can you find your way?"

"Oh, I'll manage just fine, thank you. Thank you for stopping, I, uh..." She found herself wanting to prolong the conversation but, was at a loss for anything else to say. "It was nice to meet you."

He gave her a nod and stepped back toward his open car door, then looked at her once more, just before closing the door. "The name's Mike." And with that he was gone.

Chiara, needing a few extra minutes to get her act together, leaned back against her car. She closed her eyes, took a deep breath, and shaking her head laughed out loud. "Smooth, Chiara, real smooth."

For a moment she'd felt like she was back in college, maybe even high school. Despite her most sensible self, she had felt butterflies flit their way through her insides and her pulse had picked up the pace. *And over someone I literally just met!* she scolded herself. Taking a quick look over her shoulder—on reflex looking for one last glimpse—but finding him already gone, Chiara gave her head another shake and sought to compose herself. She was here for a purpose, she needed time alone to rest and regroup. When she saw the one-page flyer stapled to the notice board, put up earlier that day by her own friend Paul, she had a feeling of certainty in the pit of her belly. This was something she just needed to do.

The flyer had been simple: Two bedroom furnished home in Came to Stay, Newfoundland, available for summer rental.

The owners, Mr. and Mrs. Boyd, were visiting their daughter in Calgary for the summer and had opened their home up to a renter. They had sent out an email to a list of their more trusted contacts. Paul had met them several years earlier while on vacation down south, and they had maintained a casual correspondence ever since. When Paul first saw the email in his inbox, he wished them well then hit delete, but something made him retrieve the email and print the flyer. Just as something made him staple it up on the board by the security entrance, and something made him mention it to Chiara that day in the gallery. Something made Chiara decide this was what she needed to do, also. However, she'd still had her wits about her, still demonstrated some of her typical tendency toward practicality in the face of uncertainty. Paul had suggested she use the trip as an opportunity to 'find herself,' to which she scoffed, requesting that he not be so melodramatic. "It's just a vacation," she had responded. "A much needed, but plain ol' regular vacation." As such, she only booked the saltbox home for a two week stretch. The Boyds had been sure to advise her that there had been no other takers for their summer rental, and that if she wished to extend her stay, she need only email them. Apparently, not many people wished to holiday in a secluded coastal village in northeastern Newfoundland.

Having gathered her senses Chiara glanced again at the ocean, promising to be back to walk its beaches as soon as she was settled, then hopped in her car, eyes focused on the house with the green roof.

CHAPTER THREE

Mike stepped out of his car and looked around. Without allowing himself to admit it, he was curious to know whether there were any cars following behind. Not yet. Slowly, he went around to the trunk, popped up the hatchback door and grabbed the tools and supplies he'd just purchased. He looked around again as he brought the door back down, attempting to be nonchalant in his demeanor. Still nothing.

With a sigh he steadied himself and turned toward the house. His own house was a yellow saltbox with three bedrooms. It was probably too much house for one person, but he hadn't been too picky when he'd moved out here from St. John's four years earlier, and it was a comfortably sized house all the same. Homes in villages like this one weren't known for their grandeur. The standard saltbox home was square and simple, intended to meet the immediate needs of its inhabitants without any frill and fuss. Simple, yet strongly built—in Mike's opinion the perfect metaphor for the Newfoundland people.

After dropping the supplies down on the porch, he went inside and, as was his habit, looked first to the group portrait hanging by the entrance wall. This was what he was about, this was his story. Making this stop every day kept him grounded, reminding him that when he moved to Came to Stay, he had truly come to stay.

"Alright then, enough foolishness. Time to get to work." Grabbing a beer from the fridge he went back out to the porch and started examining the dry rot that had formed on one of the corner beams.

He knew, though, what was coming. He knew that, had he actually wanted to be left to himself, he would have stayed in the house. He knew what he was doing even if he wouldn't admit it, telling himself all the while that fixing this porch had been his plan all along. True as that was, he also wasn't surprised when a few minutes later he heard the distinctive sound of tires turning along the gravel road. He didn't look up when the car came to a stop, didn't look up when he heard the car door open, then shut, didn't look up for several seconds after that. When he did look up, it was directly into the eyes of the person he'd been expecting.

———————

Chiara turned the car off the town's one and only through road, heading inland up a gravel laneway that gave access to four of the town's residences. She had her eye on the house with the green roof, taking it all in, sizing up her home away from home for the next two weeks. She had already imagined various scenarios for how she planned to occupy herself during her stay; drinking wine on the front porch while watching the sunset, walking the beach, collecting rocks and other washed-up sea treasures, having her morning coffee with the sea breeze on her face. She was excited to be able to provide a visual backdrop to her imagined activities, such was the artist in her, and soaked in every detail. It's only when she stopped the car in front of the Boyd home that she took a wider look around.

"You have got to be kidding me," Chiara said to herself, much too loudly, as she parked the car. With a quizzical expression on her face, perhaps a little dumbfounded, she stepped out and went around to the front of the car, staring all the while in the direction of her new neighbour. This was the expression Mike met with as he straightened up his body and slowly turned around. Meeting her in the eye he said simply, "Hello again."

"You live *here*?"

"Yes," he said, drawing out the sounds, "going on four years now."

"You didn't mention, down by the beach, that we'd be neighbours."

"True, true," he really wasn't sure why. "I suppose I figured you'd find out soon enough..." He paused at that, taking a moment to size her up in earnest. She was fairly tall and slender, but not too skinny—Mike appreciated curves on a woman. Her skin, slightly olive in tone, was remarkably clear. She had wide hazelnut eyes, richly brown, framed by strong, dark eyebrows. When he looked her in the eye it was easy to fall weak to her penetrating gaze. Her hair was down around her shoulders, dark curls being blown softly about by the sea breeze. She was wearing jeans, very well worn, and a sweatshirt that looked brand new. It had a silhouette of the island in front and the words *Newfoundland Lifestyle* written across the chest. She must have picked it up at the airport, he thought, and he couldn't deny that he warmed to her because of it. Returning to her eyes, and to his unfinished sentence, he added, "And so you have. Here, let me help you with your bags." Mike dropped the chisel he'd been using into his toolbox and headed down off his porch toward Chiara.

"Right. Yes, thank you, I'd appreciate that."

There were two suitcases in the trunk, one for her personal effects, and one filled with paint, brushes and pre-stretched canvases. Chiara fully intended to immerse herself in this rugged landscape and knew that fresh inspiration would not be hard to find. Embarrassed, though, lest Mike think that she had brought her entire wardrobe to this tiny, tiny town, she hastened to offer an explanation for the second case. "That one's filled with art supplies, might be heavy." *Smooth again, Chiara. Why do you even care what he thinks?*

Mike raised an eyebrow at the mention of art supplies, curious, but didn't comment. Instead, he led her up the steps of her own porch and placed the bags by the door. "The Boyds asked me to keep an eye out for you, in case you needed anything. They keep the spare key here, under this bench," he said as he knelt to retrieve it, letting them both inside.

"It's the only key you'll need. Kitchen's that way, washer and dryer are in the bathroom, bedrooms are upstairs of course." Mike kept himself busy as he spoke. Walking back to the door he picked up her cases and put them down by the base of the stairs. "I know they left out towels and such, you should be good to go."

For a few moments Chiara just stood there, taking it all in. Taking *him* all in. She had made a plan for herself for this trip, she had made goals for herself. She had envisioned quite clearly the days she intended to whittle away, alone with her paints and her thoughts in this harbour village. She could feel, while just standing there, her entire plan begin to unravel. And it all felt slightly beyond her control. She decided then to turn her attention toward the house.

This was not a typical commercialized vacation home, the type to take its inspiration from decor magazines and Pinterest boards. Although quite literally a beach home, there were no weather-beaten boards with *Life's a Beach* painted in large lettering, no porcelain sea stars decorating the walls. The walls themselves were painted a creamy shade of avocado-esque green, which may have been appealing to the homeowners but was generally unwelcoming in tone. The front door opened up into the living room, with a well-loved couch against one wall and an even more well-loved *La-Z-Boy* right beside it, each covered with a crocheted blanket. The opposite wall was lined with shelves which seemed to contain the entire Boyd family history. There were books of all shapes and sizes, old *National Geographic* magazines, photo albums as well as framed family photos, a few birthday cards and childhood trophies. A small television set and clock radio sat square in the centre of the entire unit. Chiara noticed small beach treasures scattered intermittently throughout, a sea urchin here, some bits of sea glass there, as though placed down on a return walk from the beach and never moved again. She examined the shelving as she passed through the room on her way to the corridor at the opposite end and, felt slightly ashamed at taking this voyeuristic glimpse into their lives. They did, she noted, seem like very nice people all around.

In the middle of the corridor was a door to a fairly large bathroom (Mike explained that it was the only one in the house), and at the end, the corridor opened up into a quaint and cozy kitchen. The room and cupboards were all painted yellow, with green vines of ivy stenciled on for added decoration. There was a window above the kitchen sink, framed by white lace curtains, that looked out toward the water—in Chiara's mind, a window with a water view belonged in every dream kitchen. In the centre of the room there was a painted wood table with four vinyl, floral-patterned chairs around it. A large bowl meant for fruit sat in the centre, safely on top of a lace doily, and hanging on the wall above, displayed proudly for all to admire, was the largest collection of spoons Chiara had ever seen. The room itself was spotless, and Chiara couldn't help but feel as though her *nonna* would feel right at home here. Having walked gingerly around, taking polite care to not disturb anything, she stopped before the refrigerator and only then did she turn back to Mike.

"Thank you, for showing me in. I don't want to keep you but, I'm just wondering if you could point me in the direction of a grocery store? Even just a corner store will do for today... In hindsight, I realize, I should have been better prepared. I didn't arrive with any food."

Mike had a look of surprise at that, as though it only just

dawned on him that there had been no bags of groceries to carry in. "Well… The nearest large grocery store is about forty-five minutes away. Not sure if that's what you had in mind, seeing as you've only just arrived."

Chiara's shoulders drooped at hearing that. "No, you're right. I have no desire to spend another hour and a half in my car…"

Nodding his understanding, Mike continued. "There's a General Store over in Queen's Cove, but, it might be hard to find if you're from away… I mean, I can take you out there tomorrow, give you a lay of the land and such. I just got back from running errands myself and I'd like to get some work done on my porch while the light's still good."

Chiara was at once grateful and disappointed. She didn't know what she would do for basic necessities until the next day, but she found herself looking forward to an opportunity to spend more time with Mike. He intrigued her, and she couldn't even explain why. Standing there in just a long-sleeve t-shirt and jeans, she could tell he was a man of simple needs, and yet, she knew also that there was a strength in him that went beyond the physical, although it was obvious that he was physically strong too. Not wanting to seem ungrateful she said simply, "Thanks, that would be great."

Mike was used to folks who spoke out, whether it was their place to or not, and being relatively reserved in nature he often wished for a little more privacy than he got, living in the country. Chiara didn't seem shy, necessarily. He could tell she was a woman who knew her own way, but she wasn't forceful about it. He liked that.

"Listen, I wouldn't be showing much Newfoundland hospitality if I allowed you to starve until tomorrow. Why don't you get yourself settled while I get some work done, and when I'm done I'll make us each some dinner. Nothing fancy, mind you, but at least you'll be fed."

"Oh, I don't want you to go out of your way. You've been helpful already."

"No, no, it's no bother at all. In the meantime, I know Bill and Cheryl would be disappointed if you didn't just make yourself right at home. They'll have some basics here already—coffee, tea—so help yourself to whatever you need." He paused there, each of them looking at each other, nothing left to say yet neither of them moving. Just as the silence reached the point of uneasy, he moved his hand through his sandy hair, giving her a sheepish grin. "Well, I'd best be going then. See you around six?"

Chiara nodded, gently. "I'll see you then."

Again, he left her. Again, her pulse quickened as she watched him leave.

CHAPTER FOUR

The morning tide was calm by Newfoundland standards, although the waves close to shore still made crashing sounds as they came into contact with the large rocks that jutted out from the ocean floor, water spraying around the solid forms. The sounds of the waves only enhanced Chiara's reverie as she sat, peacefully, on a large boulder, enjoying her first coffee of the day down at the beach. She took a small sip, comforted by its warmth against the morning chill, savouring the creamy flavours (she had easily found a canister of coffee in the refrigerator, but had experienced a slight moment of panic when she couldn't find coffee whitener of any sort—no milk, obviously, no powdered cream, no cans of evaporated milk either. A moment of inspiration came when she located a container of vanilla ice cream in the freezer, Chiara was fairly certain that this little life hack was her smartest one yet).

She sighed. She took a deep inhale of ocean air, and then sighed again. She'd needed this, more than she realized. She could feel the tension easing from the base of her neck with each crash of wave, with each seagull's call, with each soft gust of wind in her hair. She belonged to this moment, she belonged to this sea. Water had always called to her, and she would respond in a magnetic kind of way, regularly taking time to walk in parks along Montreal's canals and lakes. But nothing summoned her soul like the greatness of the ocean. It was home to her.

With another deep sigh she slid off the rock on which she was perched and started to walk. It was a clear May day. By vacation standards it was early, around seven in the morning, although the sun had risen hours ago, and she had seen several fishing boats already out at sea. There was a deep chill in the air, the kind that seeps into your spine. Her Sicilian blood retracted from the cold and she wrapped her shawl tighter around her frame. In Montreal she had needed nothing more than a light sweater or jacket and was a mere few weeks away from fishing her flip flops out from the closet, these being all she would wear until September. Winter likes to linger on the rock island of Newfoundland, however, and the May air had both a crispness and dampness to it, as air often feels during the first spring thaw.

Chiara knelt to examine some rocks, which were a lovely shade of purple, and picked one of them up, rubbing its smooth surface between her palms. As much as she was enjoying the morning, she was also distracted, her mind slipping continuously back to memories of the night before.

As promised, Mike had made a quick and simple supper of burgers, potato wedges, and a light salad. He had brought their dishes, already loaded, over to the Boyd home—a bottle of ketchup in one coat pocket, a bottle of mustard in the other—and they had eaten together at the painted table. She washed and dried the dishes when they were done—it was the least she could do, she'd said—and Mike went home shortly after, mindful of her long day of travel. It had been a short evening overall, and yet, meaningful in a way. Although they were each generally friendly, open people, their first encounters with each other had been awkward and shy. Short as it was, last night's dinner had served as an ice breaker of sorts, each of them sharing glimpses of their natural personalities, each of them accepting the other's openness in turn.

Simple as the evening had been, her thoughts were clouded

by it, and try as she did to just be in the moment at hand, thoughts of Mike were bringing her back in time. *This just won't do*, Chiara thought to herself, *this won't do at all*. The one thing Chiara knew with all certainty, the one thing she never hesitated on, was her art. She had complete confidence in her life as a painter, complete clarity of vision. Coming to Newfoundland had been meant as a break from the outside thoughts that had been creeping in and distracting her, not a break from her art. If anything, she had aspired to go on a painting streak, assuming her inspiration would be augmented by a change from the regular everyday life that had been bringing her down. Yet here she was, thoughts clouded by something new. Someone new.

"This just won't do," she said aloud this time. She needed to focus. She was here for her first love, her only passion. She was here for the artist in her. She stood back up from her kneeling position and continued her walk along the shoreline, scanning for anything beautiful that might catch her eye. Eventually, once she was tired of walking, once she'd gathered more sticks, rocks and shells than her pockets could carry, she would head back up to the house, prepare a second cup of coffee with ice cream for herself, and sit again at the painted table. This time, her sketchpad, pencils, and collected treasures would be the ones keeping her company.

Mike was eating a breakfast of toast with peanut butter while standing over his kitchen sink. It just so happened that the window over his kitchen sink also looked out toward the beach. He wondered, in an absent-minded kind of way, what she was thinking about, sitting out there on that rock. As much as he hated to admit it, he was looking forward to their drive to Queen's Cove later that morning. *Stupid*, he thought, considering that he didn't know the first thing about her. He had, however, enjoyed her company over dinner the night before.

As he watched her leave her perch on the rock and wander down the beach, he remembered that he, also, had to get moving. He still had a porch to fix, and the drive to Queen's Cove would take a chunk out of the best part of the workday. He didn't mind, didn't mind at all, but still, there was work to do.

Leaving his dish and coffee mug in the sink, he went to the entrance to pull on his work boots and fleece jacket. Grabbing his baseball cap from its hook, his eyes stopped, as usual, at the portrait hanging there. Taking an extra moment to straighten the frame, his fingers lingering, he felt his heart give its usual tug. There was nothing he could do about it, this was his life whether he chose to accept it or not.

He pulled his cap down tightly around his ears and went outside. Work. Work was what he needed right now.

Were it not for the sign above the door, the Queen's Cove General Store would look like any of the other saltbox homes in town. It wasn't directly on the main road that ran through Queen's Cove, but rather was hidden down at the end of a secondary, gravel road. Mike had been correct in his assumption that it would be difficult to find by someone new to the area. Stepping inside Chiara was hit by the aroma of fresh bread, to which her stomach immediately responded, and she looked around to spot its source. The General Store, much to Chiara's delight, was the quaintest little store she had ever been in. She laughed, heartily, at the sight of it.

Against a colourfully painted wooden interior there were tables set to one side, a bakery counter behind them, where locals could gather for a fresh cup of coffee or pot of tea along with homemade baked goods made with love by Patty, who along with her husband Burt, ran the store. Against the back wall were rows of books and DVDs, ostensibly to borrow, although Chiara wondered if they were merely decorative by this point. The main of the store had narrow aisles filled with boxes and cans of every sort, all the basic necessities, and baskets of seasonal fresh produce at the helm of each row. Chiara grabbed a wire basket, ready to explore.

"Hey, Mike! Whadda ya at?" This came from Burt, who had just come in from a back room.

"Hello Burt, whadda ya at?"

"This is it b'y. How's that porch comin' along?"

"Slowly for sure but, coming along just the same. As long as the weather holds up, I should get 'er done in no time at all."

"Well that's good to hear, my man, good to hear. So, what can I do you for this mornin'?"

"Nothing for me. This here's Chiara, she's renting out Bill and Cheryl's place while they're away. She'll be needing some supplies, I thought I'd show her the way."

Chiara, although having listened to their cheerful interaction, had only understood about half of it. Mike had a slight accent when they were together, but the thickness of their dialect, Mike's and Burt's when together, was almost incomprehensible to her. Still, she recognized that she was in the spotlight now and so politely stepped forward.

"Nice to meet you. This is a wonderful store!"

"Well it isn't much, mind you, but you can be sure to find most of what ye'll be needing. Name's Burt, that there's Patty," gesturing in the direction of the bakery counter, "you need anything 't'all you just let us know. Bill and Cheryl have been friends of ours for twenty years, they'd give us a talking to if they ever got wind of us not showing you some proper hospitality."

At that Chiara laughed. "Thank you, Burt. I appreciate that. I think I'll go take a look around." She excused herself then, heading toward the aisles. She could hear Mike and

Burt still talking,

"Have you heard from Ted 't'all?"

"No, not recently. Why do you ask?"

"Word is he'll be needing extra hands down in Bonavista, some of the crew caught a bug and he's short-handed. I wouldn't be surprised if yer phone rings."

"Is that right? Well thanks for the head's up, I'll keep that in mind."

"Speaking of which, I just got a delivery of clams out back. Interested?"

Mike looked down the aisle toward Chiara, who had been only half-listening to their conversation, wrapped up as she was in the food on the shelves, but at the mention of clams her ears had perked up and, meeting Mike's eyes, gave a wide-eyed nod.

"Yes b'y, that'd be great."

This private interaction hadn't gone unnoticed by Patty, who for four years had considered Mike the catch of the county. She made a mental note to tell Burt all about it when they were alone. Considering herself to be a good judge of character, Patty grabbed two loaves of bread and walked toward Chiara.

"Is there anything I can help you with, love? I brought you some fresh bread if you're interested."

"Oh yes, I'll take both if that's okay. They smell amazing."

"God love ya. Baked them myself just this morning."

"I have a feeling I won't even make it to the car without digging in. Having an empty fridge at the house has been driving me batty. Do you happen to carry any pasta?"

"Why of course, love. Just over here, I'll show ya."

Thirty minutes later, Mike and Chiara were headed back to the car, each of them carrying a bag of groceries. As predicted, Chiara had already broken off a large chunk of bread to snack on before offering the loaf to Mike. He smiled but shook his head. "I've never seen anyone so excited by bread before."

"I can't help it, it's the Italian in me. That store was great, by the way. We don't have small town stores like that in Montreal, nothing nearly as quaint."

He nodded. "They don't carry as much as the big box stores do, I know, but I much prefer to shop there. Burt and Patty are good people." He stopped to put on his seatbelt and start the car, then, giving her a sidelong glance said, "Italian, eh? Should have guessed by the name."

"Indeed. Chiara Costa. Doesn't get much more Italian than that. Born here, though, if it isn't obvious. My parents moved here after they were married, with my grandparents."

"You know we have a term for that? If you're not from a place then, you're *from away*. Thing is, it takes several generations before the locals around here will consider someone a Newfoundlander."

"So, I'm out of luck, then, in that case. I'll always be *from away*."

"Pretty much, yep," he joked. And then, without thinking added, "But you could still choose to stay." He could feel the colour creep toward his face as soon as the words were out of his mouth. Grasping quickly for a change of subject he decided to ask her about her life in Montreal, they had really only made small talk up to that point and he literally knew nothing about her. "So, what is it that you do down in Montreal? For a living, I mean?"

Chiara, also with a touch of fresh colour in her cheeks, was herself grateful for a concrete distraction and answered readily. "I'm an artist, a painter. I do nature paintings mostly, landscapes, but with a modern-ish twist."

"Would I have seen any of your paintings? You must be good, to be making a living at it I mean. Are you famous?"

She laughed out loud at this. "Hardly. If you were from Montreal, maybe you would have seen a piece here or there, I have a few works in public galleries. Most of them get purchased for private use, hanging in people's dining rooms or offices, never to be seen again. I make a comfortable living, though, especially since I'm on my own. I really can't complain, I get to do the one thing I love doing most in the world."

Mike was impressed by this. There wasn't a lot of 'frivolity' amongst his crowd. He knew many fishermen, day labourers, teachers and miners. People around here worked hard for their bread—a steady job was nothing to snuff at— but what the workforce lacked in imagination, the people made up for in spirit and community. A person need only to walk into their local bar or coffee shop to find someone ready with a good joke, to be met with a hearty laugh. He explained as much to Chiara, who grew thoughtful at this insight.

"I know that I'm lucky. Even by Montreal standards, Montreal being rife with artists—writers, musicians—it's hard to make a living. Most don't. I'm one of the lucky ones. But the sense of community you speak of, what I saw back there with Burt and Patty, we don't have much of that. Everyone does their own thing in the city. I could go years never knowing my neighbours, people are less willing to talk with each other. It's possible to be in a city of millions and be exceptionally lonely. There's give and take to both ways of life, I guess. Hard to say sometimes which is better."

Chiara was thinking back to her conversation with Paul weeks earlier, and the existential crisis she'd been experiencing of late. She would never regret her career path, but that didn't mean she was without regrets. "I could do with a bit of community."

Mike could feel her turning inward, her energy had changed. Uncertain as to why he ventured, "You have family around still? You mentioned grandparents."

"I do have family, yes. We're pretty close. My *nonno*— my grandpa—died ten years ago but my *nonna*'s still going strong. She likes to guilt me about not visiting enough, but when I visit, she harps on me about getting married and having babies. It's lots of fun," she joked. "And I have my parents, of course. I'm an only child so they like to pour all of their overprotective parenting energy into me—you'd never know that I'm a grown woman. They're great though. From my mom I got an appreciation for food and cooking, from my dad I got an appreciation of silence. He's one of my favourite people." She paused long enough to take a breath, then turned the questions toward Mike. "What about yourself? Do you have family around these parts?"

Mike gave her a look that she didn't comprehend. It was deep and meaningful and seemed to say so much without saying anything at all. She didn't understand the meaning in his eyes, but she understood not to say anything further. Chiara was a feeler; emotive. She felt people and situations with all her body, and she immediately felt sadness for Mike, even if she didn't comprehend why.

He turned his attention back to the car, putting the gear into park. "We're here."

She looked out the window and to her surprise they were parked in Mike's driveway, the house with the green roof awaiting next door, welcoming her home. "That was fast," she remarked, "I didn't even feel the time pass." Mike smiled, a genuine smile yet also restrained, and exited the car. She followed him to the back of the car and together they retrieved the groceries. Mike helped her carry them up to the door but, immediately excused himself so he could get back to work.

As she watched Mike head down the steps and across the bit of grass that grew between the two homes, she was overcome with the need to speak with him again, more, further. She didn't know if it was gratitude for taking her to Queen's Cove, or if she was prompted by the sadness she had felt in him—perhaps both—but just as he reached the steps of his own porch she called out to him. "I'm making *linguine alle vongole* tonight."

He turned around and stared at her, his expression blank. She waited another second then clarified. "Pasta, with Burt's clams. My mother's recipe. I figure I owe you one so, only if you have time, when you're done your work… If you're interested, you're welcome to join me."

His face softened at that. Giving her the gentlest of nods he simply replied, "Thank you," and headed up the steps.

Chiara turned, also, and headed indoors. The door closed behind her and she dropped to the floor, surrounded by groceries, and lowered her head to her raised knees. *Why? Why am I doing this to myself?* Head back against the door, she remained that way for several minutes, hoping to clear her mind.

It had been a long, long while since she'd last felt romantic notions toward a man. A long while. In her twenties she'd had a boyfriend, Ivan, for more than three years. They had had a good relationship. As graduation drew near, however, she had found herself faced with a choice. Ivan had been accepted into a master's program in Toronto, he was moving away indefinitely. He had planned for Chiara to move with him; assumed, really, that she would follow him. *You can paint in Toronto*, he'd said, *build your career there. And if it doesn't work out, there are plenty of galleries you could work at.* Chiara, however, had always been one to listen to her insides. Whether it was her gut, her instincts, or messages from the universe, her body had always spoken to her in the face of an important choice. Standing before Ivan while he rattled away his plan for them, she'd become silent as certainty set in. She would not be following him.

Her mother had been upset—not about Chiara staying in Montreal, she was over the moon about that—but it was every Italian mother's dream to see her daughter married and settled, the promise of grandchildren presumed without question. Chiara had been the first in her family to attend university, and that had made her parents proud. But in their old-fashioned minds they had assumed she would complete her education, get married, and start a family. When Ivan moved, though, and when she'd made the choice to stay behind, she had also made the choice, wittingly or unwittingly, to choose a career over family obligations.

She thought back to her conversation with Paul that day in the gallery, when she had been reflecting on her previous neighbour. It was true, Chiara had formed the opinion at the tender age of nineteen that it had to be one or the other; that women needed to choose which to prioritize between family and career. That opinion had remained a steadfast current running in her veins as she navigated her twenties. While she did make the rather unpopular decision to prioritize her career, she had promised her parents that once she had established herself, once she had built up a sustainable business, that she would return to the idea of family. She had reasoned with vigour that she didn't want to divide her energy, her focus, while she still had the benefit of youthful determination to drive her.

Yet here she was, more than fifteen years later, with the benefit of hindsight and all the wisdom gained through experience, wondering if she'd had it all wrong at nineteen, wondering if it would actually have been possible to balance it all had she been open to it, and wondering whether she had closed that door—to Ivan, to anyone—prematurely and without just cause. Wondering, also, whether she should have communicated with her old neighbour, prior to making any assumptions—and wishing she could speak to her now.

She'd meant what she had said to Mike in the car earlier, she was without community. She had her family, she had good friends and great acquaintances in the art world, but she didn't have a tribe, a group she could consider 'her people,' and what she hadn't said to Mike, but what was recently at the forefront of her mind, was the question as to whether by closing the door on family she had also closed the door on her human desire for a tribe to belong to. She was lonely, to put it plainly. This was not something she had ever allowed herself to experience, previously, and most definitely had not allowed herself to admit it, consciously or unconsciously.

But now it was staring her directly in the eye. There was something missing from her heart of hearts, and up until a few days ago she'd felt hopelessness toward ever filling that space.

Yet right there, banging away at his front porch mere feet away, there was someone interesting. Very interesting. Acknowledging that fact, though, meant facing a part of herself she had intentionally ignored, opening a part of herself that had been closed. It was painful, and uncomfortable, and as someone who had been at the helm of her own ship for so long, she wasn't used to this level of uncertainty. She didn't often lack confidence, yet here she was, sitting on the floor with bread at her feet. *What are you, a teenager?* She admonished herself as she rose, gathered her bags and carried everything into the kitchen.

She set the kettle to boil and stood at the sink as she waited, looking out at the sea. She couldn't see Mike from this vantage point, but she could hear him—*tap tap tap, tap tap tap*—and her imagination lingered on an image of him working away—his arms, his shoulders, the fit of his jeans...

"God," she shook herself out of her daydream, "get a grip, lady. It's dinner. It's just dinner." Opening a new box of King Cole tea, she set a pot of orange pekoe to steep while she unpacked her groceries. She needed to focus, she needed to relax. Running upstairs, she grabbed her second suitcase, the one with the art supplies, and carrying it back to the kitchen looked around. Within minutes she was settled on the floor in one corner of the room, canvas propped up against the wall, acrylic paints still scattered in the open case beside her, a cup of tea at her feet. This was her happy place. She was ready.

Mike had a chisel in one hand, a hammer in the other. *Tap tap tap, tap tap tap.* He was putting all of his weight into it, sweating over a couple of planks with rusted screws, wishing he had a crowbar to help pry them loose. Physically he was focused on the task at hand, emotionally he was a ball of confusion. With each strike of the hammer against the metal butt of the chisel he hoped to clear his mind, settle his nerves, go back to normal.

He didn't know what it was about Chiara that had him in a spin. Maybe it was her dark features, the long dark hair, wide, chocolatey eyes, the olive skin; all making it obvious that she was from away, all making her that much more intriguing. But it wasn't just that, though. She had an energy about her, an earnestness. She seemed to wear her heart on her sleeve, everything about her felt honest, sincere. But again, it wasn't even that. From the moment their eyes met, only the day before down by the beach, he'd felt something in the pit of his stomach that was hard to ignore. He was trying hard to ignore it, mind you, but the harder he tried the stronger the feeling became. Hence his lack of focus at the moment, the gusto with which he swung his hammer. Had he wanted to parlay with interesting women, he would not have moved out to the middle of nowhere. No, his move from St. John's had been deliberately devised for the opposite outcome, he wanted to be on his own and to be alone, no distractions. Now here he was, utterly distracted.

"Ouch! Lord Jesus Mary and Joseph!" He missed the chisel and had accidentally struck the base of his thumb. Distracted. This wouldn't do. He was considering cancelling their dinner plans, thinking up excuses he could make for not walking the twenty feet to her kitchen. He didn't wish to be rude, though, he wasn't that kind of person. Wrestling with these thoughts for a few minutes he finally made up his mind. With a confident nod to himself he said aloud, "It's just dinner. That's all. You go in, you eat your food, you go out. End of story." Decision made, Mike got back to the business at hand. He had plans for this porch and he was intent on finishing the job before month's end, summers in Newfoundland being brief and fleeting.

———————

The knock at the door made Chiara jump. She was feeling harried as she rushed to open the door for Mike, then rushed back toward the kitchen, calling over her shoulder as she went.

"Hey! Come on in. Sorry, I meant to have everything ready by the time you got here but...I got a little side-tracked. I've started though, I promise I'll have dinner on the table in twenty."

That was twenty minutes longer than he'd intended on staying. "Would you prefer I leave and come back?"

"No!" She said this with unintentional fervor and immediately adjusted her tone. "Not at all. Come in and make yourself comfortable. It won't be long."

Mike followed Chiara into the kitchen and took a seat at the painted table. His eyes followed her as she moved deftly about, adding salt, then pasta to a pot of boiling water, removing a colander filled with Burt's clams from the sink and emptying it into a simmering pan, testing the heat of the oven, then grabbing a baking sheet that had been waiting on the adjoining counter and dropping it in. He admired her ease as she moved confidently about, then chastised himself for it, and moved his eyes away. It was only then that the makeshift setup in the corner caught his attention. The canvas was obviously unfinished, yet it was striking, nonetheless. His eyes moved inward from one edge of the frame, following the lines of the composition up and up, before being carried back down again, the varying thickness of paint providing opportunities for pause and interest. Chiara was painting an image of Came to Stay, but, highlighting their laneway with its four houses as seen from the beach road. This house with its green roof and Mike's own yellow saltbox were perched at the highest point, painted more vibrantly than the others, providing a final resting stop for his gaze. On the whole it was really rather remarkable.

Chiara glanced over at Mike and caught the direction of his gaze. She had actually meant have everything picked up before dinner, or, at the very least, to turn the canvas so it faced the wall, but the paint was still wet and by the time Mike arrived she had had her hands full with dinner. She was neither embarrassed nor apologetic, she just hadn't intended on calling attention to her newest project. That said, he was looking so intently at the canvas that as its creator it was impossible for her to not feel his gaze viscerally, as though it was she herself exposed on that canvas. She didn't always mind—as a professional artist she had gotten used to putting herself out there to be examined, judged, critiqued at will by any number of people—but tonight, it was impossible not to notice the burning in her cheeks. Luckily, the hot stove she was standing over offered her a ready excuse.

Within minutes Chiara placed two steaming plates of linguine down on the pre-set table and, after returning briefly to retrieve a basket of garlic bread from the counter, took a seat beside Mike at the table. It was only then that he turned his attention away from the painting, taking in the plate of food before him.

"One masterpiece to the next. A woman of many talents, I see."

She laughed at that and, grabbing the bottle of wine from the centre of the table, said, "Here, have some wine. I can't promise that it's good, but I *can* promise that it's Burt's finest."

Mike grinned. "As much as I love to support Burt and Patty, for some things it's worth the drive to the strip mall over in Bonavista. But I'm sure this vintage of 'red table wine' will pair perfectly with the flavour of the clams." He unscrewed the twist top cap and poured them each a glass. "It's very good, you know."

"Well it's my mom's recipe, but there's really nothing to it," Chiara answered, not catching his meaning.

"The pasta too, definitely, but I was referring to the painting. You have a real talent."

She blushed. "Thank you for that. It's what I love to do. It's not done yet," she gave a nod toward the canvas, "but I was planning to leave it here, as a gift, assuming I finish it before I leave."

She meant, he assumed, for the Boyds, so he left it at that, but he felt a wave of angst at the reminder that her time here in Came to Stay wasn't infinite. *Nonsense*, his mind chimed in, *it's a relief, actually*. He sighed in an attempt to tune it all out and took another forkful of dinner.

"So, what is it that you do? Aside from renovating your home. I never asked."

Mike looked her square in the eye, then. His expression was unreadable, but for the second time she noticed just how insanely beautiful his eyes were. They were the clearest blue she had ever seen, literally the colour of the ocean on a clear day. For her thirtieth birthday she had taken a trip to the Dominican Republic, and on that trip had spent a glorious day snorkeling at a beach with the softest white sand and clearest waters. Mike's eyes transported her back to those waters, as though she could literally swim in them. They were outlined for emphasis by long, thick lashes, as if, understanding their own beauty, they decided to frame themselves. Chiara felt as though she could look into those eyes forever, yet she looked away, feeling also as though they could see right through her.

Mike was obviously hesitant to answer—he really didn't want to share too much of himself—but this topic was a relatively safe one. "Back in the day, back when I lived in St. John's, I was a skipper. There's a small fleet of boats at the harbour, they take people out, tourists and such, for whale watching tours and dinner cruises. I was one of two company captains. It was steady work over the summer, dependable work, and I got to meet new people all the time. And the view, once you're past land and out in the open water, there's nothing like it. Takes my breath every time. In winter months we'd shut down so I would take odd jobs as they came, that's pretty normal around here. And that's pretty much what I do now, too. In the summer I'll go out on fishing boats when they need an extra set of hands or, work odd construction jobs as they come along. In the winter I might help with the snowploughing…" In his thickest drawl he added, "I goes where I'm needed most."

She smiled. Chiara didn't know if she would ever get accustomed to the local lingo, but she found it both amusing and delightful. "You're a wanderer then, a roamer."

"Not necessarily by choice, but I suppose that's accurate."

Feeling as though they were on a roll, Chiara continued her quest to feed her curiosity. "So, what do you prefer? The fishing boats or the tour boats?"

Mike replied plainly. "I prefer to be on the water. Wherever that takes me." It was the simple truth of the matter, but for Chiara's sake he continued. "I got into the touring business as a practicality, it met my needs at the time, better than the life of a fisherman did. Over time, though, I came to find that it really suited me. The boats got larger, more challenging. And obviously, the larger the boat, the larger the crew, and that suited me well, too. More than anything, the slow, quiet rides out to sea, having the opportunity to be an observer of nature—watching whales, that was always my favourite part—it checked every box for me. I really enjoyed it."

Mike paused. They had finished eating by then and, wishing to remove himself from the centre of conversation he rose to clear the table. "Well, I'd say it wasn't necessary, but that was too delicious of a meal for me to have passed up. Thank you for inviting me."

"Honestly, Mike, it was the least I could do. You've been

very kind." As she spoke, she rose from the table to collect the assorted cutlery and glassware. Coming suddenly face to face —or perhaps, in the moment when they each unexpectedly realized that they were face to face—an audible silence fell between them. Lasting longer than was reasonably comfortable, it was Mike who was the first to speak.

"I, uh... It's been a really long day. I'm beat. Unless I can stay to help you with the dishes..." Chiara recognized that he wasn't offering so much as being polite.

"No, not at all. You go ahead. I'm sure you're exhausted." Mike carried the stack of dishes to the sink, then excused himself, promising to see himself out.

Alone in the house once more, Chiara, who had been left still standing at the painted table, plunked herself down and poured another glass of wine. The dishes would wait.

———————

Back at home, Mike stood, leaning against the inside of the front door, staring at the portrait on the wall. He leaned there for a long, long time, taking it all in, recalling each memorized detail to mind. When his phone rang, it took a few rings for him to shake himself off enough to answer.

"Hello?"

"Hallo Mike? It's Ted. Whadda ya at b'y?"

"Hey...Skipper. Nothing much. What can I do you for?" Mike was absent-minded but trying his best to hide it.

"Listen, I have a rig leaving in the mornin' and I'm down a few men. I was hopin' ye'd be interested in a few days' wages?"

Mike looked out the door's window at the house next door, and back again to the wall before him, stopping there. There was a firmness in his voice as when he replied.

"Yeah, Skipper...timing couldn't be better."

CHAPTER FIVE

Chiara parked her car in an unofficial spot at the side of the road. There were a handful of other cars scattered around the area, parked wherever was convenient. Upon waking up that morning she'd made the hasty yet firm decision that she needed to get out of the house, needed to leave Came to Stay altogether, at least for a few hours. She was desperate for time alone to reflect, regroup, and recentre. She needed to do more of what she'd come to Newfoundland to do.

It had been a restless sleep and she was groggy as a result but, pulling her backpack from the passenger seat and turning toward the ocean breeze that bounced off the cliffs around her, her hair dancing around her face as a result, she could sense her cells rejuvenating.

"Doris and Emily would approve."

Doris McCarthy and Emily Carr were Chiara's gurus—even if only in spirit. Both were iconic Canadian—female—landscape artists, respected for their craft. Both were a little eccentric and more than a little spunky. Neither, as it happens, ever married. Chiara had done extensive research on both artists while in university and had felt a kinship with them that remained present throughout her career. She liked them as people—at least from what she knew of them—and she respected them as artists, considering them grandmothers of Canadian art. She would often read their writings when she was in need of inspiration. On this day, what Chiara needed most was their spunk, and as she set out, she said a little prayer to them as her spirit guides, begging for a boost.

Chiara had chosen a hiking trail that would take her across seven kilometres of cliffside, ending at a lighthouse at the top of the same rocky cliff. The trail itself was hardly a trail. Wide enough for one person, it was mostly just beaten down grass inconspicuously marking the way. It followed the cliff's edges closely, making the trail more interesting than if it had simply followed a straight line, but also making her feel as though she were living on the edge—figuratively more than literally—which gave her a rush. The perceived danger was actually quite minimal, however looking down at the giant rocks jutting out from the water, and the massive waves crashing down over them, was both mesmerizing and terrifying.

The vista from this vantage point was magnificent, though, and Chiara couldn't get enough of it. All of it. The view, the sea breeze, the smell of the salt air, the sound of the waves. Looking inland, she saw a pasture on the other side of the road where several cows were either grazing or lying about.

"Happiest cows in the world right there."

Mike had left home around three in the morning, anxious to make it to Bonavista before sunrise. He was looking forward to the quiet ride and the still of the night. Aside from the possibility of running into a moose, something that was always a lingering precaution in these parts, the roads were completely and peacefully his own. A man could hear himself think, there on the open road.

Whether or not he wanted to hear his own thoughts, that was another matter altogether.

Looking through a telescope that was stationed by the lighthouse, Chiara squinted for a better look at the small rock island just a short distance away. It took her a moment to make out the various shapes and shades coming into focus and, gave an excited *Oh!* once she realized the island was covered in puffins.

"What's the other bird out there, the white one with the yellow head?" She directed her question to an elderly couple standing at the rail beside her, having eavesdropped enough of their conversation to understand that they were locals.

"Those are gannets, dear, ocean birds. Look a bit like seagulls from this distance, except for their yellow heads that is." The couple then pointed to a little red boat that was out on the water, several kilometres away. "That's one of the whale tours out there. It looks like they may have found a whale since they're sticking to that area, we were just hoping to catch a glimpse."

Chiara turned the telescope in the direction of the boat and scanned the surrounding waters. A moment later she spotted a white spray of water reaching high up and out from the ocean's surface, water from a blowhole she realized, and following that the whale's gleaming grey body protruded from the sea—just its back, curved and strong—remaining above surface for just a few seconds before descending again.

"There she blows!" said Mr. Nice Couple.

"What a tease!" Mrs. Nice Couple joked in return, causing Mr. Nice Couple to give a hearty chuckle.

"Ah well. Best we be going, dear. I doubt we'll see her surface again."

Chiara gave them a friendly wave and watched them wander off with a smile on her face. The smile slowly faded as her mind travelled from the whale to the tour boat to the kind couple, to thoughts of Mike. She'd done a good job of shutting him out of her mind all day, but this gentle reminder had put her right back at that kitchen table the night before. Up until last night, she had thought that perhaps the attraction was purely one-sided, or that that were each just playing shy. But then he'd left so abruptly… And now he was gone altogether. During her restless night, as she was returning from the bathroom, she had heard a car door slam and the turn of an engine. Glancing outside, she caught sight of the red taillights of Mike's hatchback, just before they disappeared into the dark of night. *What is he so afraid of?*

The morning was still quite young as Mike took the last sip of coffee from the cap of his thermos before tightening it back on. The water was unusually still, the morning sun casting a golden glow over the port side of the boat, as well as making millions of tiny little shimmers across the ocean surface. Despite the sun and calm winds, the temperature was frigid. The still steaming coffee had helped to warm his insides but hadn't done much to thaw his fingers. Rubbing them together then bringing them to his lips for a blow of warm breath, he recommenced the tedious, yet gratifying, task of mending trap netting. Mike enjoyed tasks like this—straightforward, uncomplicated, with a direct beginning and end. There was something satisfying about being able to complete a task in a measured and calculated way, crossing it off a mental checklist once done.

He had been, for as long as he had remained in the position, a well-esteemed skipper, specifically due to his steadfastness and surety of mind. His premature retirement had left many disappointed, but everyone who was anyone had completely understood his decision. On mornings such as this one, however, he missed his old life. He missed the sea.

Returning to his netting, he allowed both eyes and mind to wander as his fingers worked. In the distance he saw a small circular ripple made from a fish that had jumped to the surface. He watched those ripples, emanating outward slowly, slowly, slowly. *Like a heartbeat*, he thought. *Until, of course, it stops.*

———————

There was a small diner roughly midway through the seven kilometre hike back to her car. Given the lack of housing in the immediate area, the diner seemed to exist purely to serve travellers like her, making their way to the lighthouse at the top of the cliff, trying to encapsulate the immensity of the panorama into one memory. The fresh air and exercise had expanded her appetite and she forced herself to limit her order to a club sandwich and fries. Moving to the back of the diner where the windows were largest and views greatest, she found herself a table and sat with a thud. She had only, just in that very moment, realized the depths of her fatigue.

She remained unmoved for a few minutes, mind blank, the rhythm of her body shocked at the abrupt stop. A waitress placed a can of *Canada Dry* and a clean glass on the table and Chiara took a long and satisfying sip, the boost to her blood sugar helping to focus her mind. With considerable effort she retrieved her sketchbook and a pencil from her backpack and began a light sketch of the view from the window—including the window—while she waited on her food.

Whereas she had been exhilarated when she set out that morning, she was now exhausted and feeling rather pensive. Chiara had a true artist's spirit. She was a feeler, shy but emotive, excitable and full of ideas, but she was also prone to melancholy when she allowed herself to kneel vulnerably before certain unanswerable questions. Chiara was a fighter, however, with a very determined personality. Growing up, her dad loved to give her a knuckle job across her head, calling her *testa dura*, hard-headed, as he went. Even Paul, her close friend, would affectionately roll his eyes at her and say in his most sarcastic voice, *Mais oui ma petite tête dure*.

Her dilemma at the moment, and for the past month if she were being honest, was that all the separate parts of herself were at odds with each other. The more she tried to bring about peace, the greater the tensions became. This hike was meant to quiet the noise—heck, this entire vacation was meant to—however Chiara was finally resigning herself to an honest admission; no amount of hiking or travelling or eating or painting or running or chasing was going to fix this. Only she could fix this. And she could only do that by finding the courage to remain still, to finally surrender to her emotins. The question remained, was she courageous enough?

———————

"MacCloud! Ted says he needs ya tomorrow as well, we're goin' out again. You good with that?" This came from Ron, Ted's right-hand man and for Mike, a friend.

Mike, who had been stacking lobster traps, paused with a trap in mid-air, turning so he could face Ron. "Yes, my man. Sounds good to me! I could use the extra day."

Ron looked him over, skeptically. "If ya don't feel like driving back 'n forth, y'er welcome to my sofa. Wife's outta town and I have me a hankering for a cold pint and a hot plate of fish 'n chips."

Mike usually preferred the comfort of his own home, his own bed. He didn't mind the long drive home after a full day of work, and the longer drive back after just a few hours of rest. This time, however, the chance to remain away was particularly inviting.

"You know, Ron, I thinks that's a fine idea."

———————

Chiara was brushing her teeth when she heard her phone ring. She'd received the odd text since her arrival but hadn't been expecting any phone calls just yet. Turning on the tap, she bent forward to allow some water to stream directly into her mouth, then, spitting quickly, she grabbed a hand towel and rushed out of the room to find her phone.

"Hello?"

"Good morning, beautiful. How is my favourite lady on this glorious day?"

With a glance out the window, Chiara shrugged. "Less glorious on this end, I'm afraid. Newfoundland isn't known for its weather." To say the morning was overcast was an understatement. A grey gloom hung over the entire village, the fog so thick that the horizon had disappeared, creating one seemingly impenetrable wall of cloud. The fog rolled inland off the beach below, its thin wisps moving progressively toward her, or so she felt. What a contrast to yesterday's fine day. "You're calling me sooner than expected. What's wrong?"

She heard an overexaggerated gasp through the line and she could visualize Paul feigning shock into the phone. "Does something have to be wrong for me to call you?"

"Usually, yes," she replied with mock sarcasm. Her friendship with Paul had always been based on their mutually dry humour, so she was caught off guard when his tone turned suddenly serious.

"In all honesty, I was just thinking about you, out there on *the rock*, and something told me that you were in need of a friend. I just had to call." The line went silent for a moment, and Chiara wasn't sure if he was allowing her a chance to speak, or if he meant to continue. Either way, she wasn't ready to respond. "So, how are you doing, anyway?" he ventured.

How *was* she doing? She didn't even know. She was fine, in the most literal sense. Physically strong, she had her health

and her wits about her... She knew this wasn't what Paul was
asking, but she was unusually insecure in her search for an
adequate response.

It was the eve of her fortieth birthday. She had never been
so *freaked out* by what was essentially just a number. Another
year had passed, just as any year, and it had been a successful
year at that. Professionally, she was at the top of her game.
The Montreal Gazette had published a two-page exposé in
their Arts & Culture section. A curator in Toronto had
contacted her and their communications were moving progressively toward them hosting a one-woman show in their
gallery by autumn. She was even anticipating a trip west to
B.C. by the end of the year. She had nothing to complain
about. Yet, as she had hinted to Paul the last time she saw
him, she had a distinct sense that there was something lacking
in her life, and she had pangs of regret, worrying that she'd
closed one door too many, and that they'd remain forever
shut.

"The issue, then," Paul was saying, "is that you pigeon-
holed yourself, all by yourself, and now you don't know how
to get out of it."

"Pretty much, yes. And I'm feeling so much angst around
it, almost suffocated by it. For the past twenty years I have
identified as an artist and only as an artist. But…I think I need
more in my life. Love. Companionship. Family. I've been
skirting around if for weeks, pretending this was just a phase,
or that my birthday was just stressing me out. Pretending I
could paint my way to a better place. I can't, though. These
are things that I want. Except now that I've finally allowed
myself to accept this as truth, I feel even more depressed
about it. I can't just *poof* love into existence. And I'm forty
now, you know. My baby-making years are dwindling."
Chiara let out a deep sigh, one Paul could feel from the other
end of the line, and his heart went out to her.

"Want my sperm?"

"Get out!" Chiara cried, but he knew as he heard her

laughing that his remark had done the trick.

"Why don't you take yourself out on the town? There's got to be a tall, dark and handsome fisherman just waiting for a beautiful and successful lady to come his way."

Chiara's mind went to Mike, Mike with the perfect height, perfect arms, perfect shoulders and, of course, those eyes. Mike who was reserved, but kind. Mike, who had disappeared into the night and had still not returned.

"No, there isn't. There really isn't."

———————

Ron and Mike were seated at a white vinyl-top table, the metal pedestal legs uneven, causing the table to kilter back and forth whenever either of them moved. Mike folded his cardboard coaster and bent underneath, jabbing it under one of the legs. Rising, he tested his work, then, satisfied that the coaster was doing its job, he looked Ron square in the eye.

"Why do I have a feeling as you've got somethin' on yer mind?"

"Do you?" Ron countered. "Do I?"

"I can't say as I know just what y'er talking about b'y." It was true, he didn't know what was on Ron's mind, but Ron was someone he trusted, someone whose opinion he valued, so he knew that if Ron had something to say it was likely worth hearing.

The waitress returned with their beer. Momentarily confused by the missing coaster, her eyes darted about, finally settling on a spare on the neighbouring table which she grabbed with one hand, balancing her tray with the other. She dropped it in front of Mike with some annoyance, but her tone was chipper as she served the men.

"There y'are loves, be back soon with your food."

Once alone, Ron continued. "I was just wondering why you're here."

"How do you mean?" Mike didn't know where Ron was going with this but was beginning to feel mildly irritated.

Ron began. "Not two weeks ago ya told me that you weren't going to take any jobs 'til yer renos were done, yet here y'are. Now I knows ya don't need the money so, I find myself asking *Why?* And I knows ya hate staying in town, yet here you are…"

"You invited me!"

"Yeah, I did, with every expectation ye'd turn me down like ye always do. Don't get me wrong, I'm happy to have you—I loves ya like a brother, you know that—but in the years I've known ya, you've never seen the inside of my house."

Mike knew he was right about that, so responded by taking a long, deep drink from his beer. But Ron recognized the delay tactic and so persisted.

"What I think is that y'er avoiding something, and now I'm curious as to just what it is y'er avoiding."

Being confronted with it in that way, directly, face to face, there was no denying what, or whom, he was actually avoiding, and his face flushed involuntarily.

"Ah, it's a woman then."

The waitress returned with their food then, and Mike used the opportunity to deflect Ron's attention, uttering his thanks to the waitress and examining the plate before him. Two pieces of heavily battered haddock glistened on one side of the oval-shaped plate, the other half covered in hand-cut fries. At opposing ends of the dish were tiny metal bowls filled with tartar sauce and coleslaw, respectively. This was good, wholesome Newfoundland fare, comfort food, and Mike's belly was already responding.

"Dig in?"

The men picked up their forks and began, each silently agreeing on food before conversation. During this time Mike's thoughts roamed to Chiara, her long dark curls, her wide, round eyes, the way they sparkled when she was excited about something. He thought to her slender body, how she carried herself with ease—she was comfortable in her own skin and it showed—and he thought to her smile, her lips, slightly plump and pouty, but in a cute way. Her lips. Her lips.

He glanced up and caught Ron examining him again. "Alright, alright. It's a woman," he said, resigned.

"So, what's the problem? She doesn't like you?"

"No, nothing like that... I guess the problem is that she might."

"You're not attracted to her then?"

"No... I am..."

By this point Ron looked exasperated and didn't mind showing it. "Seems to me half the men in Newfoundland would be happy to have your problem."

"You know it's more complicated than that, Ron. When I moved out here four years ago, it was because I had made up my mind to avoid people and relationships and all the things that go along with them. I was happy to hole myself up in my little house, and I'm still happy for it. Now, I've come to make some good friends along the way and that's okay, I appreciate all of you. But a woman, Ron, I'm not ready for that. I don't think I'll ever be. I swore off women completely and I have no intention of changing my mind."

"But it's been four years, b'y. Just like ya said. A man can't be alone forever. Eventually you're going to have to reopen that part of yourself. It's what she would have wanted."

"You don't know that."

"I didn't know her, but I know you. And I know you would have had yourself a good woman, a generous woman, and that kind of woman would never have asked you to hole yourself up like a hermit for the rest of your days. That I do know for sure, and so do you."

Ron was right, again—not that Mike was planning to admit it. Whatever she may have wanted for him, he never thought he could want it for himself. Not without her.

For his part, Ron was convinced that his friend was selling his life short. Ron could count on one hand the number of people he could trust his life to, and Mike was one of them. That Mike didn't seem to value his own life was irritating to Ron. Wanting to press the point—with a look toward future opportunities—Ron tried a different tactic.

"So, Ted got to talking today. He's thinking of expanding the fleet. He also wondered if you might want to come on permanently—not just as crew, but as a business partner."

"Whoa." Mike hadn't been expecting that.

"Just giving you a head's up, it's something to think about. You'd have your own boat, your own crew, plus have a hand in growing the business. You'd finally have a chance to really stretch out those sea legs of yours. Tell me that isn't better than what you've been up to?"

The question was rhetorical, but Mike questioned him anyway. "What have I been up to?"

"Exactly my point, b'y. That's exactly the point."

Martyn came all the way from Canada to London just to see me and with him lugged that great love he had offered to me out in Canada and which I could not return. He warned of his coming in a letter, carefully timed to be just too late for me to stop him even by wire. For I would have pleaded, "Dear Martyn, please don't come." ...

But Martyn on the platform at Euston Station was like a bit of British Columbia, big, strong, handsome. I had to stiff myself not to seem too glad, not to throw my arms around him, deceiving him into thinking other than I meant...

I showed Martyn every sight I thought would interest him. We went to the theatres. Martyn liked Shakespearian plays best, but it did not matter much what the play was, whenever

I took my eyes off the stage I met Martyn's staring at me.

"What's the good of buying tickets!" I said crossly—
"you can see my face for nothing any day." He asked me on
an average of five times every week to marry him, at my
every "No" he got more woebegone and I got crosser. He
went to Mrs. Radcliffe for comfort and advice... I wished she
would tell him how horrid, how perverse I really was, but
she advised patience and perseverance, said, "Klee Wyck
will come round in time." ...

"Come home, Emily; marry me; you don't belong here."

"I can't marry you, Martyn. It would be wicked and cruel,
because I don't love that way. Besides—my work."

"Hang work; I can support you. Love will grow."

"It is not support; it is not money or love; it's the work
itself. And, Martyn, while you were here, I am not doing my
best. Go away, Martyn; please go away!"

"Always that detestable work!"

Dear Martyn, because he loved me he went away.

"Martyn's gone back to Canada."

Mrs. Radcliffe's eyes bulged.

"When are you marrying him, Klee Wyck?"

"Never."

Mrs. Radcliffe jumped to her feet. "Little silly! What more
do you want? Is it a prince you wait for?"

"I wait for no one; I came to London to study."

Slowly Chiara closed the book, hugging her cup of tea
closer to her chest. "I should really just get a dog."

———————

Ted cancelled their second excursion in the end. The fog had
rolled in thick during the night and a man couldn't see five
feet in front of him, let alone any boat or rock that could be

potentially in their way. Ron had suggested that Mike stick around until the fog cleared but Mike had decided to get on his way. With no work to do it was time to go home.

The drive was a difficult one and his eyes were getting tired. The roads here were winding, following the curves of the coastline, and with the thickness of the fog it was all he could do to stay between the lines. Luckily there weren't many other cars on the road.

He had just passed a sign indicating the turnoff to Shimmering Cove, a neighbouring town, and took a brief second to roll his head to each side, giving his neck a chance to release some tension. He turned back to the road before him and refocused his eyes. His low beams were on, and he suddenly noticed the light reflecting back in an unusual way. *Eyes.* He could barely see the body of the beast, it was so consumed by the fog, but he knew it was there. Thinking quickly, he slammed on his horn to shake it from its standstill—knowing from experience that it would be mesmerized by the headlights—as he swerved his car to the left. It was a deer, he could see now, and had it continued in the direction it was faced all would have been fine. But the deer was skittish, afraid, and indecisive. Turning suddenly, it began to run in the opposite direction. Mike hit his brakes and swerved hard to the right. The road at that point was curving rather sharply, and Mike's sudden action had driven him directly off the road and well into a ditch.

Lucky bastard. He was directing this at the deer, who had gotten away unscathed. Assessing his situation, he added, "Arsehole!"

Knowing there was nothing else to do, Mike called for a tow truck and settled in for a long wait. His days as a captain had taught him to always plan ahead, to be prepared, and he had taken up the habit, in winter months, of keeping spare items in his backseat; a shovel, a wool blanket, a toque and mitts. Given that no one ever sat in his backseat everything was still there, and, having shut off the engine, Mike reached back for the blanket to keep him warm. He was tired. The difficult drive had taken a considerable amount of energy out of him, and he decided to use the time to rest his eyes. He turned on his hazard lights, lest the tow truck drive by and he was asleep, and grabbed the knit hat, tucking it down low, covering his eyes.

Sleep came quickly to him, as did dreams; lucid dreams, the kind to make him think he wasn't sleeping at all.

He was standing near the crest of Signal Hill in St. John's, looking down over the harbour and city with all its beauty and colour. The hike up had left him out of breath, panting, and a little clammy. He was searching for something he couldn't see, or was it someone? He wasn't sure. Turning to look uphill he saw a female figure standing on a large bit of rock jutting out from the surrounding cliffside. She was wearing a dress, the colour of the ocean, and he knew he had finally found what he'd been searching for. He turned with resolution and began the steep climb to reach her. He found, however, that with each step her face changed. One moment fair-skinned with red hair, the next, olive-skinned with dark hair. He continued taking steps toward her, hoping to have her face come into focus, hoping to know just who it was standing there, waiting for him. But no matter how high he hiked, how many steps he took, he could never reach her. He was sweating by then, desperate, and in his desperation, he called out to her. "Who are you? Please, tell me. Show yourself to me!"

As in a movie, as a camera changes its perspective, zooming slowly inward, so did the lens of his dream. Slowly, slowly, blocking out more and more of the surrounding landscape until it was just her, her body, her—not yet in focus—her—a little more—her. Finally, he could see her face.

Mike woke with a start, his heart pounding. A shrill *beep, beep* came from outside and, lifting his hat, he could see that the tow truck, having just arrived, was backing itself up to a more convenient position. He was clammy, as in the dream, feeling the perspiration from his hands to his feet. Absentmindedly he rubbed his face between his hands, trying hard to shake the sleep from his eyes.

Home. He needed to get home.

CHAPTER SIX

Chiara was sitting cross-legged on the floor, having decided to begin her day with coffee and paint. She was reminded of her university days, painting on the floor of Ivan's dorm room into the wee hours of the night, only to delicately carry still-wet canvases to class the next morning. That was ages ago, a lifetime ago. She could never have imagined how far she would come. And now it was her birthday. And she was resolved to enjoy every minute of it.

She had lingered in bed upon waking up that morning, remembering the pity party from the day before, allowing yesterday's mood to roll around in her head. Her *nonna* had always told her, 'You can't always choose what the universe will throw at you, but you can choose how you handle it. Always keep going, keep moving forward. Life will catch up.' Her *nonna*, who had known no small amount of advers- ity in her life—not the least of which was war—knew what she was talking about.

Chiara decided, right there in her bed, that it was time to put her big girl pants on. She understood that it was one thing to have a problem and ignore it, but it was another thing to understand, acknowledge, accept, and then move on. Her head was not in the sand, she wasn't practicing avoidance. But she acknowledged that there were some things within her control, and some things utterly beyond it; these she decided to surrender to the universe, to allow her little dilemma its own time and space to achieve its own resolution. She decided to continue on with her life.

She had a very loose plan to head down to the beach after breakfast, collect more beach treasures, and perhaps find a local restaurant where she could eat some yummy seafood for dinner. Her mouth was salivating over thoughts of a traditional boiled lobster dinner, when she heard a loud but brief knock at the door. Surprised, Chiara put down her brush and stood up, taking care not to knock over her coffee, and walked the short hall to the living room.

She saw Mike through the window well before she reached the door and stopped quite suddenly in her tracks. "What…the…heck." Her heart was beating loudly, she could feel it pulsing in her eardrums as she opened the door. She was sure that he could hear it too.

"Good morning."

"Good morning."

Silence.

Mike eventually ventured to break through the awkwardness of the moment. "I was wondering, if you aren't busy that is, whether you're free for the day. I was thinking of taking a drive down to Trinity, I'd appreciate the company if you're interested."

Silence, again. Chiara realized that it was her turn to speak but was entirely confounded and it caused her to be tongue-tied. She recognized that it had been a while since she'd had anything even remotely resembling a romantic relationship, but she had never before experienced this level of hot and cold from a man. Her first impression of Mike, the impression that remained, was that he was the strong and silent type, sure of himself, someone you could trust to keep you safe if needed. She could trust him with her life, but not yet with her heart that was beating at full volume. Still, she enjoyed his company, and who better to experience Newfoundland

with than with someone who lived there. As much as she had
planned to spend the day on her own, she did feel pangs of
relief at the prospect of sharing the day with someone
instead. Making up her mind she replied.

"That sounds great. I'll just pour my coffee into a travel
mug and grab my purse. Should I bring anything?"

She noticed a brief expression move across Mike's face
as she responded, one of relief but also...fear? Nervousness?
Yet he remained steadfastly composed.

"Nah, just yourself. I've already packed some things into
the car." He started to head back down the steps but stopped
himself, looking back at her quickly he added, "Actually,
you'll want to bring a coat."

The drive to Trinity was a quiet one. Chiara entertained
herself by watching the passing scenery in all its beauty. As
opposed to the previous day, the sun was shining brightly, the
light bathing over the treetops which glowed as a result. She
was forming a deep appreciation for the natural ruggedness
of these lands; untouched, unmanicured, unpretentious. While
there was a lot that Chiara appreciated about Montreal—the
art culture with its galleries and music festivals, the multic-
ulturalism, especially when it came to food; she loved
eavesdropping on conversations between people speaking
both French and English interchangeably without skipping a
beat, and of course her friends and family were there—but
nature spoke to her on a deeper level, and she often felt it
necessary to leave the city. Several times a year Chiara
would rent a chalet in the Laurentians, north of the city,
choosing a place nestled deeply in woods and by a lake,
sometimes just for a weekend but more often for a week at a
time. She would call this her *forest bath*, adopting the
Japanese term as her own, and as a landscape artist she

considered it necessary to feed her inspiration in this way. But Newfoundland's rocks were rockier, its waters were bigger and louder, its trees were...tree-ier, if that was a thing. More dense, more shades of green. The weather was unpredictable, the island itself was alive. This place resonated with her and—as much as Mike confused her—she was grateful to him for inviting her to explore more of it.

"Here we are."

They had pulled up to the harbour, the picturesque town of Trinity behind them. She saw several boats lined up along the pier and a small crowd was gathering by one of them. Mike opened his car door and looked over at her, motioning with his head.

"C'mon!"

She followed him down to the pier as they joined the waiting crowd. Mike left her side, walking up to a man in a vest the same colour as the boat. He obviously worked there. The man was laying down a walking plank, but when he looked up and saw Mike approach his face broke out into a wide smile. He dropped what he was doing to greet Mike, the two of them shaking hands in an affectionate way. She couldn't hear their conversation, but Mike said a few words and put a strong hand on the man's shoulder, the man in turn gave Mike an undeniable look of respect. Their private greetings over, Mike turned saying, "Wells I best be lettin' ya get back to work b'y," and he returned to Chiara's side.

"That there's Finn. He used to work on my crew, down in St. John's. Now he manages his own operation here in Trinity from May to September."

"His own operation? You mean whale tours? Are we going on a whale tour?" Her pitch became progressively louder with each question. Mike hadn't said anything about his plans for the day, Chiara had simply been following along. It was only in that moment that she realized what the crowd was waiting for, and why they themselves were standing in line. It was the second time that morning that

Mike had surprised her to the point of speechlessness and he laughed shyly at the expression on her face.

"Well you can't come to Newfoundland without seeing whales and icebergs, so whales and icebergs are what we're going to see."

Chiara was so excited that her impulse was to hug him, but she used all her willpower to refrain from doing so. Still, she gave him a smile so wide, so genuinely happy that for a moment, he himself was speechless.

Finn untied the rope that was blocking the plank and the crowd began to board. The boat was a zodiac vessel, small and low to the water. "Is this safe?" Chiara asked, swept momentarily by a wave of nervousness at the idea of being out on the wide Atlantic in such a small vessel.

But Mike gave her a reassuring nod. "Safe as any other, and if we do see a whale, there's no better view." He motioned for her to board ahead of him.

Chiara nodded her understanding and stepped on board. She was the first in her row, closest to the edge of the zodiac. Mike sat beside her, necessarily close to make space for other passengers, and she was distinctly aware of every inch of their bodies, from their shoulders to their knees, as they touched. She could tell that he was just as aware of their proximity as she was, both of them looking elsewhere, pretending not to notice.

The zodiac moved slowly away from shore, then picked up speed as it reached open waters. The boat moved between waves, over waves and through waves, and Chiara could feel each bump, each lull, each rocking to and fro. She gave a brief horrified thought to seasickness but, commanded her stomach to cooperate. Her stomach, already aflutter over sitting so closely to Mike and the excitement of their excursion, was sufficiently preoccupied and agreed without question. That resolved, she looked out at the horizon, at the sheer vastness of the ocean.

To Chiara, the ocean was a mystery that people either

embraced or feared. No one knew just what was lurking below the surface, no one could tame it. You were either awed by this, drawn to its magnetism, left wanting to learn its secrets, or, you remained land-locked, feet steady on the ground. Chiara was moved by the ocean every time she was near it but, being out on the water was electrifying. She closed her eyes to the salty breeze, feeling ice cold drops of water spray across her face as the zodiac hit across waves. A sense of peace came over her, a happy calm created from the perfection of the moment, and her lips involuntarily turned upward.

With the sudden sense that she was being watched Chiara opened her eyes and glanced shyly at Mike. His blue eyes, deep and intense, were set on her face. Having been caught staring at her he chose not to look away, but rather smiled at her in an appreciative way. His body relaxed next to hers, as though he had been sitting tensely until that very moment. Her body responded. Chiara hadn't even realized that she'd been tense until she suddenly wasn't.

The boat had been following the general contours of land from afar. Changing direction slightly as it followed around a bend, they came up on an iceberg, still at some distance, but the sight of it took Chiara's breath away. Chiara was not known for appreciating anything winter-related, Sicilian bloodline and all, but the iceberg was glorious. Strong lines moved up and down, jutting sharply in different directions. Chiara tried to follow the contours of the massive shape with her eyes, only to become lost in its peaks and valleys. She tried to memorize the varying shades of white and blue— aqua, turquoise, periwinkle—with hopes of bringing this memory to canvas in the near future. The zodiac circled the iceberg a few times, allowing everyone ample opportunity to admire its grandeur, then continued out to sea. They were hoping, still, to catch a glimpse of a whale.

The tour in its entirety was scheduled for two hours, and they needed to save time within that to carry them back to the Trinity harbour. The collective energy of the boat's pass-engers was shifting in degrees from excitement, to hope, to resignation. Finn, who'd been on hundreds—if not thousands —of excursions knew that anything was possible and worked hard to keep spirits high and jovial, telling jokes and stories in his thick, East Coast accent, while simultaneously letting it be known that they were mere observers of the sea, with no control over the wildlife itself. Most people had their eyes glued to the water ahead, searching for telltale sprays, and one passenger, an elderly gentleman sitting near the back, was certain he had seen one to the west of their current location. Being generally in the direction of their return, Finn said, in a voice that made everyone feel he was doing everything possible to give them their best experience, "Let's give it one more shot!"

The zodiac blasted forward for a few kilometres before slowing down again, eventually coming to a complete stop around the area where the gentleman had seen the water spray up. The water was fairly still here, the zodiac rocking ever so slightly. Everyone was silent, watching, not yet wanting to admit that they had already given up hope. They remained that way for three minutes…four minutes…five minutes.

She wasn't sure what made her do it, but Chiara leaned sideways in her seat, gently, and looked directly down into the water. Right there, right under their zodiac, was a hump-back whale. Startled, Chiara grabbed Mike's arm tightly, and he also leaned over to see what had captured her attention. The whale swam low around the boat, then came back around, pausing for a while, as if to allow Mike and Chiara the chance of a better view. Chiara felt frozen in time. She wanted to speak but couldn't. She wanted to inform the other passengers but, didn't want to scare the whale away. She was also, somewhere in the back of her mind, worried what would happen if everyone tried to cram to one side of the small boat. The humpback was easily twice the zodiac's size. With her free hand she gripped her seat, as though that one hand was enough to keep the boat steady and sturdily above water. She could feel Mike's body pressing solidly against her, feel his breath near her face as they both continued their watch, she could smell his aftershave as it mixed in with the salty air. They remained that way—for how many heartbeats she didn't know—but although time had stopped for Chiara and Mike, it was the whale that had finally had enough, turning away from the boat, curiosity satisfied, directing its body lower and lower, until it was gone.

"She won't come back up for air for at least another twenty minutes," Mike's voice sounded breathless as he said it. "And who knows where she'll be when she does come up again." Straightening herself up and turning to him, they shared a look of dazed amazement over what they had just experienced, mixed with a tinge of guilt for the other passengers whose eyes were all still fixated further out.

Finn finally had to announce that it was time to head back and there was a collective shuffling as everyone—having been sitting at the edge of their seats—settled back for the ride. With no intentions of stopping again before the pier, the zodiac picked up speed and Chiara's hair began to fly around her face. As they rode, she realized that she was still clasped on to Mike's arm. He'd kept his arm still, not wanting to disturb her, and she gave him an apologetic smile as she let go, using the opportunity to tie her hair back in an elastic to hide her embarrassment.

Disembarking back in Trinity, they overheard a couple in front of them sharing their mutual disappointment at not having seen any whales, to which Mike and Chiara could only share a knowing smile.

"Are you hungry? I brought sandwiches."

They walked until they found a bench and sat side by side, Mike's opened backpack between them. He pulled out two bottles of water and two sandwiches. Chiara eyed the pinkish meat pressed between two slices of white sandwich bread. Each slice of bread had been dressed with butter and mustard, respectively. Their sea adventure had built up her appetite and realizing that she was famished, she took a large bite before asking, "What is it?"

"What is it? Seriously? It's bologna! Do you mean to tell me you've never had bologna?" Mike was whole-heartedly surprised, letting all guard down for the sake of one of his favourite foods.

"I mean, I've *heard* of it obviously…but I've never had it. I grew up in a pretty Italian-centric neighbourhood. The closest we came to bologna in our lunches was…mortadella? Is mortadella to Italians what bologna is to Newfoundlanders?"

She was teasing, mildly, just as Mike was feigning disgust as he answered with a very curt, "No. No no no no no no no. Bologna is very versatile, you see. You can fry it, you can eat it as a side with eggs, you can chop it up and add it to your macaroni and cheese, you can even eat it frozen. There's like, literally nothing you can't do with bologna. I mean, I'd even go so far as to call it our national food."

Chiara was biting the insides of her lips, trying hard to suppress the giggles that were dying to escape. "So, what you're telling me then, if I'm to understand this correctly, is that by eating this sandwich, I am essentially, you know, becoming a Newfoundlander." She laughed as she said it, then louder as she looked at him. Mike was nodding solemnly as though to express the severity of her statement. He broke his charade though, rather suddenly, as an idea very obviously had sprung to mind.

"We gotta go!"

"What? Uh… Okay."

She wasn't sure why, but Chiara helped Mike pack up their lunch items and followed him away from the harbour. Mike led Chiara into Trinity on foot, up one road and across another. Each street was peppered with more of the colourful housing common to Newfoundland, shades of blue, yellow, red and green. They passed several small businesses on their way, each with its own distinct promise of an authentic

Newfoundland experience. Having arrived at his intended destination, Mike opened a door and held it for Chiara to enter, following from behind.

They had entered a pub, a very warm, very cozy pub, with wood tables and private bench seating, wood paneling on the walls and low, warm lighting. A few fitting relics decorated the room—antlers, lanterns, coils of rope and an old wooden helm—and there were touches of brass lining the bar, softening the glow that much more. There was nothing modern or trendy about this space, making Chiara like it immediately. Mike led her to one of the tables then excused himself, leaving her to get comfortable on one of its benches.

She watched him move across the room, allowing herself the opportunity to appreciate his features. She wasn't sure of Mike's exact age but guessed that he was in his early to mid forties. She considered this for a while, marrying the age with the image before her. He held himself with the maturity born of years of experience, but still possessed the physical strength of youth. He was attractive, very attractive. The more time she spent near him, the more attracted she became. He stopped at the bar, looking back over his muscular shoulder at Chiara. She blushed, thankful for the dim lighting, and pretended to rest her head on her hand to hide her school-girl smile.

The bartender, an older man in his sixties with grey hair and an impressively bushy moustache, approached Mike and the two of them chatted. There were a few hand gestures, and at one point they turned simultaneously to look at Chiara, then turned back to each other with a laugh. It was becoming difficult for her to hold back her curiosity. The bartender poured two pints of beer from one of the taps, then, with a nod to Mike, exited through a doorway behind the bar. *Kitchen?* she wondered. Mike had a wholly satisfied expression on his face as he returned to the table with the two pints.

"I hope you like beer—I'm sorry, I should have asked first."

Taking the cold glass from him she replied. "Yes, beer is great... I mean, thank you. It's just... Mike, what were the two of you talking about just then?"

He smiled mysteriously and took a sip from his pint. "Let's just call it a birthday surprise."

"Wait! How did you know that it's my birthday?"

There was no way that Chiara would have shared that tidbit of information with Mike. She didn't mind that it was her birthday, or the idea of aging—aside from, of course, her minor existential crises of late. In fact, she had never let a year go by without celebrating her birth in some form or fashion. But sharing a birthday with someone she barely knew... What she hadn't wanted was for him to be obliged to her, or uncomfortable in any way. Apparently, she needn't have worried.

"The honest truth is that I looked you up online. After seeing the canvas in your kitchen the other night, I—I guess that I was just curious to see more of your work. Chiara Costa has quite the online presence if you didn't know, your birthday kind of just popped out at me."

She blushed again. It had never occurred to her that he could be curious enough to look her up. That it was interest in her work, especially, that drew him to learn more was particularly touching. She looked into his eyes from across the table, and he into hers. The energy shifted, inexplicably, between them—a palpable feeling of connectedness gave rise. Her mind went blank, her heart stopped, her breathing turned shallow, and she was conscious of a faint ringing in her ears. That look, those eyes. *Oh God, help me.*

And from across the table, equally captivated—and equally terrified—by this look that neither one of them could ignore; *Lord luva God, I'm in trouble.*

A noise from behind the bar broke the spell, for which they were each grateful. The bartender had returned. He looked to Mike first, as though for confirmation, and came out from behind the bar carrying a tray. Mike turned to Chiara and gave his hands a clap.

"So!" he began.

"So?" she replied, hesitantly.

"So. We have a long-standing tradition here in Newfoundland and Labrador—one we reserve specifically for mainlanders such as yourself," he said with a wink. The bartender placed the tray on the table before them. Chiara examined the contents then looked up at the bartender, then to Mike, then back to the bartender.

"What am I supposed to do with that?"

Mike cleared his throat, for the most part to hold back the giggle that was working its way up. Dawning his thickest possible accent, he began.

"There's only one true way to become an honorary Newfoundlander, if ya want to be by the book with nothing half-arsed about it. We have to Screech you in."

Chiara interrupted. "Screech me in? What does that even mean?"

Mike held up one of his hands, comically indicating that this wasn't the time for questions. "Now put on that there hat," he ordered.

Chiara took a yellow rain hat off the tray and put it on. She was becoming increasingly amused by Mike's enthusiasm. Although she had no idea what to expect from this little ceremony, she could tell the men were having great fun at her expense and she happily played along. "I feel like Paddington Bear in this hat."

"That's a Sou'wester, it's longer in the back to keep yer neck dry out on the high seas. Now I'm goin' to ask ya a serious question and I'm goin' to expect from ya a serious answer. Are ye ready?"

"Ready!"

Mike continued. "Would you like to become a Newfoundlander?"

Chiara was about to respond, but the bartender leaned down low by her ear and whispered. She nodded, then looked at Mike and voiced loudly, "Yes b'y!"

He found her attempt at an accent incredibly adorable and laughed despite himself before continuing on with the ceremony. "Now, *is* you a Newfoundlander?"

Again, the bartender leaned down with a whisper. Chiara listened, but this time turned suddenly to the bartender and stared him in the eye. "You want me to say *what?*" The men laughed again, thoroughly enjoying themselves. The bartender leaned down once more, taking his time to enunciate the words. "Okay…" Chiara said this to the bartender, in a tone of uncertainty, then turned to Mike to repeat the phrase. "Indeed I is, me ol' cock! And long may yer big jib draw!"

This set Mike in a howl of laughter, so contagious that Chiara and the bartender followed suit. The only other patrons in the pub were two men, also in their sixties, sitting at the bar. They became curious at the festivities and, grabbing their pints, walked over to corner table. It took only seconds for them to clue into the scene and they became equally giddy, unable to hold back the laughter in their eyes.

Composing himself finally, Mike went on. "Normally at this point we'd pass around a plate of bologna—so you could eat something Newfoundland, you see—but seeing as ye just came from eatin' a bologna sandwich we can skip that part. Now you have to kiss something Newfoundland."

There were now four men surrounding Chiara, three of whom were in their sixties and would have loved nothing more than a kiss from a younger—if not young—pretty woman. And Mike. Handsome, handsome Mike. Chiara experienced a moment of panic over the recipient of her kiss but this was quickly quashed, however, as Mike picked a frozen codfish off the tray and held it up so that she and the fish were face to face. She tilted her head slightly to the side, looking around the codfish so that she could look Mike in the eye. "You're pulling my leg!"

"I swears to ya I'm doin' no such thing. It's an integral part of the ceremony."

The other men began to voice their agreement, eager to see if she would actually do it. Chiara looked at the old men and realized that this was likely the best entertainment they would have all day, perhaps even all week. Trinity was a small and quiet town, tourist season wasn't yet in full swing, and she was sure that their enthusiasm was amplified by this small break from their regular day. She didn't mind giving them something to cheer for, and she didn't have the heart to let them down. She looked at Mike, then looked at the codfish, its eyes still glassy despite its frozen state. Giving her head a shake of determination, she closed her eyes as tight as she could, puckered her lips and leaned in, kissing the fish on the mouth as quickly as possible.

The group erupted into loud cheers. Smiling widely Chiara asked, "Is that it? Am I an honorary Newfoundlander now?"

Mike was clapping his hands but stopped to remove one last item off the tray. He placed a shot glass on the table before Chiara, filled to the brim with a golden-brown liquor. "Now you have to drink something Newfoundland. A glass of Screech—rum, basically—and ye'll be officially Screeched in. It tastes like the devil, and it'll hurt like the devil going down too. But, down the hatchet she goes!"

Taking his direction Chiara picked up the shot glass, lifted it in the air with a slight nod toward the men, then brought it to her mouth, downing its entire contents in one go. Again, the group erupted in animated cheers, visibly impressed with her abilities, and Mike beamed at her willingness to put on a good show. Chiara could feel him staring at her with smiling eyes. She didn't want to turn her head, didn't want to meet his gaze, as she was already flushed and didn't want to make it worse in front of the entire group. She waited until the bartender collected everything on his tray, taking his leave, followed by the other men after several pats on the back and raising of their own pint glasses in her honour. She finally turned her head toward Mike, whose eyes were still set in her direction.

She was swimming again in the intensity of their blue waters, it hadn't been hard at all to fall in. But she had trepidation, too. It had only been five days since Chiara had first set eyes on Mike. While the attraction had been immediate, it had been an emotionally tumultuous few days, and Chiara admittedly didn't know anything at all about him. There was a darkness about him—rather, a shadow that followed him—and it made her nervous to not know more, understand more, about this man before her. When she looked into his eyes, though, in the few naked instances such as this one—guards down, authentically themselves—she knew instinctively that he was good, deeply good, and made the decision to trust him.

"That was a lot of fun. Today was a lot of fun." She truly meant it and hoped her voice conveyed that message.

Mike nodded, calmly, slowly. "To be completely honest, I can't remember the last time I had such a good day. It's been a while. A long while."

Tempted as she was to ask him questions, to know more, she also feared that the shadow would return. He was open to her right now, he wasn't hiding. She wasn't willing to jeopardize their almost perfect day. Instead, she circled back to the Screech ceremony. "What did that mean? Big jib draw …et cetera." She was too embarrassed to repeat it.

Mike, on the other hand, felt no qualms and repeated proudly, "'Indeed I is, me ol' cock! And long may yer big jib draw!' It means, Yes I am my old friend—ready to become a Newfoundlander, that is—and may your sails catch wind. Or, may you always be fortunate, to put it another way."

Chiara picked her coaster off the table and began to turn it between her fingers. It helped to keep her fingers occupied when she was nervous. "And is it a for real thing, this Screeching in? You weren't just pulling my leg?"

"No ma'am! It's a tradition that has withstood the test of time. You still come from away, mind you, you'll always come from away, but—you'll always be welcome."

Chiara smiled, understanding his meaning. "I'm happy to hear that. I love it here, I really do."

Mike paused, as though choosing his words carefully, then continued. "It's fun and games, I know. We have a lot of fun at other people's expense, but we also have a lot of fun at our own expense. There are a lot of stereotypes about us as a people, and we could fight them, but that's just not our style. Newfoundlanders prefer to have a sense of humour about themselves. We've experienced hardship, historically. We aren't the richest province and we definitely cope with the harshest weather. But when it comes down to it, to deny the stereotypes would be to deny the traditions that formed us. Instead, we ham it up, celebrate them, and give ourselves a good laugh in the process. Plus, you'll never meet kinder people, and that's a fact."

Mike's pride in his homeland, his people, his nation, was showing across his face. "Could you ever see yourself living anywhere else?"

"What? And be a mainlander?" A look of mock shock crossed his face and Chiara held up her hands in apology. "No, I don't think so. This is my land. These are my people. This is who I am." He spoke in earnest, his eyes, once again, expressing the truth in what he said. She watched him as he spoke, the slight crinkles in the corners of his eyes, his angular jaw, which became firm when he was discussing something serious, and his pointed nose leading downward to his kind mouth, kind lips…

Chiara felt a sudden urge to kiss him.

———————

"Hi, Ma."

"Happy Birthday, sweetie. Sorry I'm calling so late, we didn't forget about you. Promise."

"That's okay. I was out all day anyway, I just got home a few minutes ago."

"Did you have a good day?"

"I had a *great* day!"

She could hear her mother take a deep breath before responding. "That's good, honey. I'm happy to hear that."

"You okay, Ma?"

"Yes, I'm just tired."

"Is Dad around?"

"He's…already asleep."

"Okay. Why don't you go to bed too, Ma? We can talk more later."

"Okay. Goodnight, honey."

"'Night, Ma."

"Happy Birthday."

Sofia hung up the phone and wrapped her blanket more tightly around her legs. She was tired. Bone tired. She had spent so much time sitting up in the armchair beside her husband's hospital bed that the days and nights were beginning to blur. She wished that Chiara was here with her, to be with her, to help her, to keep her company and just to give her a break when needed. Despite frequent calls and occasional visits from neighbours, friends, and her elderly mother-in-law, there was no one she could lean on to help her through the mental and emotional roller coaster of these past several days. She felt so alone.

Giovanni's health had deteriorated even more rapidly than the doctor predicted. It had been a matter of days before they moved him into the hospital full time, and only a few days after that before they began to notice a drastic decrease in his bodily functions. He was still cognitive, however, and very aware. Try as she might to convince him to call their daughter, he remained steadfast in his decision to leave her out of his illness. As much as Sofia had been the force in their relationship, when Giovanni decided to dig in his heels there was nothing she could do. *Testa dura.* Chiara hadn't gotten that particular trait from nowhere.

Sofia leaned over and gently rubbed her husband's arm. Giovanni. *Her* Giovanni. The only man she had ever loved. They had been through so much in their forty-three years of marriage, including a stillborn child, the loss of three of their parents, and a move to a new country—new continent, new world. Everything they had done, they had done together. She didn't know how to go through this without him.

"Mrs. Costa? Can I get you anything?" One of the night shift nurses had stepped in—Nurse Rose, one of Sofia's favourites—interrupting Sofia's train of thought.

"No, thank you, I'm fine."

"Why don't you go home for a few hours? A full night of sleep and a hot shower will do you some good."

Sofia didn't disagree, she craved her soft bed and warm duvet, she craved the comfort of home. But what was home without Giovanni in it? Looking at her husband then, with his pale skin and chapped lips, the hollows of his eyes dark and sunken in, she could scarcely see the strapping young man she had married so many years ago. Her heart squeezed tightly in her chest. She could not leave him.

"I'll be okay, Nurse. I prefer to stay."

CHAPTER SEVEN

The urge to kiss Mike lingered for days to follow.

They spent the following four days together. One afternoon hiking in the surrounding woods, another, hammering side-by-side at Mike's porch. He would go over and watch her paint, sitting himself at the painted table with the local paper, pretending to work the crossword puzzle as he watched her through the corner of his eye. She would follow him down the long laneway toward the beach each evening, making a daily habit of watching the sunset together. There were no streetlights in Came to Stay so when dark came, it came quickly. They would always head back up the hill toward their respective homes just as darkness fell over the tiny town, the rooftops fading quickly into the darkening sky. Then they would sit out on her stoop or his and chat for a while, quietly, allowing themselves to blend into the quiet of the night around them. All of Came to Stay went dark by nine each night. The town's residents were older, mostly, and went to bed early. With only the scarce porch light still on, and the light of the stars upon them, Mike and Chiara used these still moments to get to know each other better, deeper, feeling comforted—perhaps protected—by the darkness of night.

Mike learned that Chiara had been married to her work for

the past twenty years, and that she hadn't had many serious relationships in all this time. She admitted to having a date now and then, sometimes casually dating the same person for months at a time but, specified that she had never before encountered anyone with enough pull to outweigh the attention she gave to her work. She spoke from her heart about her fears around relationships and how they could affect her work, that one of her main concerns had always been the distraction that romance could bring. She was honest.

"It's different for a woman with a career goal. At least, that's my perception. You're expected to drop everything to raise your family. And not just that. When maternal instincts kick in, it would be hard for a mother not to *want* to be there, taking care of her family. And I wasn't willing to put myself in a position where I'd have to choose between loves, prioritize one over the other. Because either way, one would lose out, and I'd be torn up about it. My career is so, so important to me. It's been my life. Lately though, I've been having regrets, wondering if I've been wrong about my way of thinking all along. It's been weighing on me, *a lot*, to be honest. It's not that I never wanted kids…"

Mike liked to listen to Chiara speak, the soft sound of her voice blending with the noises of nature at night. The cadence was relaxing to him. He realized, also, that he'd been lonely. He hadn't been aware of it but, having Chiara there with him filled a void he hadn't previously acknowledged. Once he did acknowledge his loneliness, he grew hungry for more of her companionship. He asked many questions, about her family and friends, about life in Montreal, and Chiara would willingly answer, happy for the companionship he offered in return.

She told him that he reminded her of her father. "I mean, aside from the obvious cultural differences, your characters are similar."

"In what way?" he asked, wanting to know more of her perception of him.

"You exude an inner strength, but without any machismo or ego. He's the same. I've never once heard him complain about any of the hardship he experienced. He takes after my *nonna* in that way. If it ever bothered him that he had to work hard jobs, long hours doing physical labour to support his family, I never knew about it. He was there for every graduation, every art opening, every *anything* that was meaningful to me. But he has never asked for anything in return. For birthdays and Christmas—forget it. He just tells me to save my money. As a kid, I would look at him and think he was the strongest man on the planet. I once watched him carry an entire sofa by himself, on his back, from the back of his truck right into our house. No word of a lie. He was like... Did you ever watch *Little House on the Prairie* growing up? He was like Charles freaking Ingalls to me. My own Charles Ingalls. Kind. And strong. That's how I see you, also."

She paused there, allowing her silence to take shape while her thoughts wandered freely. When she broke the silence after several minutes, her tone had a slightly melancholic twinge to it. "It's hard seeing him age. I'm an only child, I can't help but think about how devastated I'd be if I didn't have my dad in my life. Any of them; my mom, my *nonna*. They're all I have."

Mike had gone silent at that, it was impossible for Chiara not to notice. It had not gone unnoticed that he preferred to question her about her life, rather than open up about his own. She didn't want to pressure him into opening up about whatever hurt he had experienced in his life—for it was also obvious that Mike hurt—however she was not willing to ignore it, either. She placed a gentle hand on his arm, just enough to feel the strength of his forearm under his fleece, and cocked her head in question. Mike shook his head in response, not ready, and simply replied with, "I was an only child too. I know what you mean." Then, redirecting, "What about your mom? What's she like?"

Pensive, Chiara took her time to respond. "What isn't she

like? She's Superwoman. I think I've always had a secret insecurity that I would never be able to fill her shoes, there's nothing that woman can't do. She has dedicated her life to her family, gladly, with gusto, without any need for attention or praise. She's strong. She's an amazing cook—she makes virtually everything from scratch. And she has a wicked sense of humour—her belly laugh is infectious. We quarreled a lot when I was younger—I thought I knew everything—but now, we couldn't be closer. She's my rock."

Had it been anyone else, Mike would have excused hims-elf from such conversations. Being privy to other people's family ties was the last thing he felt he needed. With Chiara, however, it was less about her family and more about her relationship with them—he was interested in who she was and where she came from, it told him a lot about her as a person. When it came to Mike, however, Chiara had to rely on her intuition.

It's only when they spoke about their hometowns that Mike would really open up, prideful of his roots and home. "Folks around here still call me a townie, because I hail from St. John's. They like to tease. But they're good, real neighbourly folk. They'd do anything for me if I asked, and I would for them. Winters are hard out here, and most of these guys," he waved his hand in a wide gesture, "are older. I help where I can, plough their driveways, take requests when I'm riding into town. In return I'll often find homemade meals at my door—the women can't resist feeding the one and only bachelor in town."

Chiara laughed at that. "Except for the winter part it sounds idyllic."

"Aw, it's not that bad."

"I don't winter very well."

"I'm lying through my teeth anyway. It is actually that bad."

She laughed again. "I don't get any of that in Montreal though. I've lived in the same condo for years and I couldn't tell you anything about any of my neighbours. People keep to themselves, barely a nod or a hello. I'm sure there are some places on the island that are more neighbourly—"

"Oh, that's right. I forget sometimes that Montreal is an island, too."

"Yep. And very different from the rest of the province. Maybe, how you think about Newfoundland versus the mainland?"

"We take no issue with Mainlanders. We just know what it takes to be from here and to live here; it takes grit. We have a lot of history and it makes us prideful people. You won't catch us whinging and whining, you know?"

"I respect that, I really do. This place is honestly growing on me a little more each day. Montreal—it's multicultural, and I love that about it, but Newfoundland is multi-colourful, vibrant, and that speaks to me, too. I feel like I could easily spend entire summers here, with the beach and the ocean, and the quiet... They serve me well."

"And winter?"

Chiara laughed, and with an assertive nod responded, "Cuba."

Mike laughed in return. "Another island, must be in your blood."

"Or my destiny. Not just to live on an island, but to be one, too."

"Well," Mike replied, looking intently in her direction, "'no man is an island.' Or so I hear."

"I guess we'll find out…"

Chiara and Mike loved these little nightly chats, but inevitably the May air would become colder as the night went on. Chiara would begin to shiver through her coat, her fingers numbing, and they would rise and say their good nights. At no point did either of them suggest going indoors to continue their conversation in the warmth of his home, or her temporary abode. They were each too conscious, too anxious, about what could come between them, unspoken, in close proximity and under the cover of night. She would smile at him, or he would give her slender arm a light squeeze, and they would go their separate ways. Pausing, always, for a last look in each other's direction before heading indoors.

———————

Five days after Chiara's birthday, and ten since her arrival in Came to Stay, Chiara heard a light knocking at her door as she was preparing a late breakfast for herself. She had already been down to the beach and back, and had included another urchin shell, dried starfish, and purple and grey rock to her collection of beach items now piled into the fruit bowl on the painted table. She'd been humming to herself contentedly, feeling full and whole and at peace, something she hadn't felt in a long time. Paul had been right after all, this trip had been precisely what she needed.

She had just taken a shower and was wearing a bathrobe that likely belonged to Bill Boyd, making up in comfort what it lacked in femininity. It hung loosely on her tall and graceful form, but in such a way as to suggest that what was hidden was worth seeing. This is how Mike saw her, when she opened the door in response to his knocking. He stood speechless, undeniably stirred by the sight of her, his eyes widened in pleasant surprise at her disheveled state.

"I, uh... I'm headed down to Queen's Cove to pick up some supplies. I just wondered if you needed anything?" He left it as a question in his voice. What he really wanted was for her to join him, but he was too taken aback by her natural beauty to get the words out of his mouth. He shunned himself in his mind, telling himself, *You're a grown man, MacCloud, pull yourself together!* But he found he couldn't help it. He didn't know what it was about Chiara, specifically, but just being around her made him weak.

Luckily, Chiara was of a similar mind. "Would you mind if I tag along? I would love the drive." That settled, Mike left her to dress while he returned home for his wallet and keys. He walked right past the portrait on the wall as he gathered his things, his mind fully consumed by the image of Chiara in the bathrobe, hair loose and wet, skin still glistening. It had been so long—too long—since he'd last thought about a woman in that way.

The drive to Queen's Cove was a silent one. The air between them felt thick, and they each decided independently that words would only complicate matters. Unlike the previous days, where they had experienced an obvious mutual attraction, and had enjoyed time spent getting to know one another better, this day was different. Palpably different. Sexual, without either of them intending it to be, and neither of them knew quite what to do about it.

The sounds and smells of the General Store were a welcome distraction. Mike immediately went in the direction of Burt, standing behind the cash register, chatting with a few other men. Chiara went in the direction of the tables by Patty's baked goods. Patty herself was there, wiping down the tables with a wet towel. She turned at the sound of footsteps and seeing it was Chiara let out a happy exclaim.

"Why hello, love. So happy to see you back! Are you having a good visit then?"

Chiara couldn't help but look in Mike's direction as she responded. "Yes, I'm having a lovely time. It's been very good for me."

Patty, always keen when it came to matters of the heart, did not let that glance go unnoticed. "Here, love. Take a seat and let me pour you a cup of coffee—no, I insist! I would love for you to try one of these muffins I just baked. It's a new recipe, you'll be doing me a favour if you could taste-test for me."

Patty went behind the bakery counter for a minute and quickly returned with two steaming mugs of coffee held together in one hand, and a plate with two still-warm muffins in the other. The two women sat at one of the small round tables and Patty set everything before them. "There now, I was in need of a break anyway. Now we can relax and enjoy some girl talk. Once those men get to talking about fishing and such, there's no telling how long they'll be. And they say women talk too much. Ha!"

Given that Patty hadn't stopped talking since they sat down, Chiara found this last bit to be particularly amusing. Patty was a cute, bubbly, woman in her mid to late fifties. She had a grandmotherly vibe to her, and she made Chiara feel immediately comfortable. She was also, Chiara noted, sharp as a whip. Chiara wasn't entirely surprised when, nonchalantly picking up her cup of coffee but looking Chiara directly in the eye over its rim, she asked the question Chiara sensed coming.

"How are things with Mike?" She took a sip then, as if the question had been completely casual and innocent. Chiara hid an uncontrollable grin that was directed as much at Patty's prying question as it was at her accent. Patty pronounced some "th" words with a hard "t" sound, so that *things* came out sounding like *tings*.

"With Mike? How do you mean?" Chiara might not have been from a small town, but she knew enough about small towns to know that personal business tended to become everyone's business. And she knew enough about Mike to know that he liked his business to remain as private as possible. Besides that, in truth, there was nothing to share. She and Mike had known each other for less than two weeks, they had a growing friendship. What more could she say?

Patty wasn't having any of it. Rolling her eyes, she looked at Chiara and said, "Don't you try telling me there is nothing goin' on between ya's now. I saw the way you looked at each other the last time you were in and I went home that night and I said to Burt, 'You know Burt, a fine lady like that is exactly what Mike needs.' Burt bein' Burt, he just grunted and nodded—he doesn't like me to meddle. And I don't meddle, mind you. I just see what I see, and I know what I know. And what I know is that our Mike is as fine a man as we have around here, and I hate to see him wasting away all by himself in that yellow house, not sharing his life with anyone. Just the thought of it makes my heart ache. He doesn't deserve to be alone."

Patty stopped for a breath and another sip of coffee, and Chiara took the opportunity to fish for answers herself. "My understanding is that Mike chooses to be alone. It must be what he wants, no?"

Patty gave her a look that was somewhere between pity and dismay. "You can't expect him to know what's best for him. Especially given his situation."

At this Chiara's curiosity was officially piqued. "His situation?"

"He didn't tell you, did he?" Chiara shook her head no. "Ah, well then, I suppose it's not my place to be sayin' anything. Tragic though. Just tragic."

Chiara looked at Patty, flabbergasted that she would carry the conversation so far and then not provide Chiara with the piece of the puzzle that had been missing these past few days, the history of Mike. Chiara wasn't going to ask for it though, not wanting to be the one to break Mike's trust, and also not wanting to provide Patty with any more ammunition for her imagination.

Patty made an abrupt decision not to share any further details, so took to questioning Chiara about her life. In some ways Chiara felt like she was being interviewed for a position she hadn't officially applied for, but Patty was sweet, and she only had Mike's best interests at heart. *And she is a damned amazing baker.* With a bite of muffin in her mouth there was absolutely nothing that Chiara could fault her for. *She's smart,* Chiara joked internally, *she knows it's her secret weapon.*

Having finished the muffins and coffee, and the interview apparently over, Chiara and Patty rose to clear the table.

"Thank you so much, Patty. That was absolutely delicious."

Patty took Chiara's long, thin hand between her own soft, round fingers and gave it a squeeze. She gave a quick look in Mike's direction before speaking. "Y'er deservin' of the best, lovey. So is he." Taking the dishes from Chiara's hands she turned and headed behind the bakery counter.

Standing alone Chiara closed her eyes. She woke that morning feeling fresh and clear, and only a few hours later her mind was clouded and confused. Is this what she had meant by distraction? Is this what she had been avoiding for so long? She didn't know what it was about this day but, opening her eyes and looking across the store at Mike, it had everything to do with him. As if sensing her looking at him Mike shifted his glance, catching her eye. They held each other's gaze for a while, then Mike turned back to Burt and the other men, excusing himself so he could attend to his shopping. He walked over to the tables and stopped in front of Chiara.

"You looked like you were having a good heart to heart with Patty."

"It was enlightening."

He raised an eyebrow at that, but she shook it off. She wasn't about to divulge any of what Patty had said, Patty was watching them from across the counter and Chiara knew it. Mike turned and caught Patty looking at them approvingly and, closed his own eyes with a blush. He suddenly knew exactly what, or whom, the ladies had been talking about. Opening his eyes, he gazed down at Chiara, standing before him with her face flushed and pretty. He sighed, making the decision to fully surrender to the powers that be. Instinctively, she followed suit.

"Are you ready to do some shopping?"

"Am I ever!" She laughed, and he joined in, both profoundly relieved. It seemed that whatever tension they had felt between them since that morning had suddenly vanished. In its place was an open and honest acknowledgment of their

closeness, an unspoken understanding that they were connected, and they moved throughout the store that way.

Patty watched them from her perch, occasionally glancing
at Burt with an all-knowing smile. They seemed to be moving
in unison, in tune with each other as they walked, talked,
shopped. *Ahh, young love*, Patty thought. It didn't matter that
Mike and Chiara were in their forties. In a fresh relationship,
all people are the same as far as Patty was concerned. It was
her favourite part of any romance, so full of hope and
promise. Burt was forever catching her reading what he
called 'those cheese-filled romantical books' in the back
kitchen while waiting for her goods to bake. Occasionally
fanning herself she would claim it was a hot flash or the heat
of the oven, but Burt always knew she was reading
something steamy and would chuckle as he passed through
the room. Burt and Patty had been married for over thirty
years and while it was no longer young love, it was the kind
of love that Patty wished on everyone. The kind of love she
had been wishing on Mike for years. She had been blessed
in her life, she was certain of that, and she sometimes took it
as her personal mission to encourage this blessing on others.

Mike and Chiara emerged from the aisles, their baskets
full, and headed over to Burt at the cash.

"All done, then?"

"Yes b'y, what do we owe ya?"

Burt rang up their items while chatting pleasantly about
the weather, it was turning out to be an unusually warm and
sunny day, and on a whim threw a bag of marshmallows into
their bag. "Don't know what you have planned for the day
but ya may as well make the most of it."

They thanked him, waved goodbye to Patty and headed
outdoors.

"Feelin' rather romantical yerself then, are ya?" Patty
said to Burt with a wink.

Back in Mike's car, he looked at her before turning the
key in the ignition. "So, how 'bout it?"

"How about what?"

"Marshmallows." She continued to look at him, so he added, "Beach? Bonfire?"

Her eyes lit up as she clued in. "Yes!"

They made a plan to picnic down on their beach in Came to Stay. It was quiet there, with only twenty houses in town it was rare to run into Mike's neighbours, especially before summer kicked in. Mike offered to make it an authentic beach meal, a fish fry or mussel boil over the bonfire. However not having any fresh seafood on hand meant a return to Burt's or making another stop further away. They were both eager to return home and to the beach, so they quickly agreed on a less fanciful meal.

They had found their footing back in Queen's Cove, had released whatever tension was between them, and continued to move as though in harmony. Mike went into his yellow saltbox for food and condiments, Chiara went into her saltbox for beverages and a blanket. They emerged at the same time, met each other on the driveway and walked down the lane.

As expected, the beach was quiet. Remarkably quiet. The tide was low, the waves were calm, and the seagulls remained out at sea. Mike showed Chiara what types of driftwood they would need, and together they scoured the beach, amassing an impressive pile of logs and branches both thick and thin. Mike arranged them in a triangular fashion and, taking matches from his pocket set to work on lighting the fire. As he did this Chiara sought out two long and pointed sticks, then pulled a large log over to the fire and sat down. Despite the high sun and calm wind, she still sought warmth from the heat of the fire.

Mike leaned back against the log next to Chiara. He raised a knee, resting an arm on it, the other leg stretched casually in front. He was relaxed, Chiara observed. She followed his gaze into the fire, and together they sat there, watching the flickering flames as they grew higher and stronger. When it was hot enough Mike took one of the largest logs from the wood pile, adding it to the bonfire for lingering heat.

"Hungry?" he asked.

"Starving."

They skewered hot dogs onto the long sticks Chiara had scavenged and sat side by side as they cooked them over the open flames. With nothing but plain buns, ketchup and mustard with which to dress them, it was easily the tastiest hot dog she had ever eaten. Chiara could taste the bonfire, the salt air and earthy beach with each bite, and went in for seconds and thirds, matching Mike hot dog for hot dog until they both leaned back, stuffed. Chiara fished two bottles of beer from her tote bag and offered one to Mike, which he took gratefully. They sat like that for a while, nursing their beer, not looking at each other but feeling each other's presence.

Chiara could have gone on this way for hours, she thought. Mike, however, had reached a decision. It was time to break the relative silence of their afternoon, time for him to break the silence he'd been keeping for years.

"I, um… I was married. Before."

CHAPTER EIGHT

Mike didn't know that he was going to open up to Chiara
until the moment he did it, but he felt certain that it was the
right thing to do. The past days together had been the most
satisfying days he'd had in a long while, and this day, in
particular, he felt so close to her. Connected. In truth he
wanted to kiss her, but he couldn't do that without first
explaining his past, the past that he had held steadfastly
between them since day one.

"I told you already that I lived and worked in St. John's.
I was raised there. My parents—I was an only child, like
you—they were professors at Memorial, the university there.
Good people, kind people. Smart people. We were a close-
knit bunch. I think they always assumed that I would be an
academic like them, but the sea called to me from a young
age and I just wanted to be on it and part of it. But I also had
Trish to think about too.

"Trish and I had been high school sweethearts, like you
hear about in the movies, you know? We were always
together, never even considered separating or trying things
out with other people. She was a real sweetheart. She had
long red hair, lots of freckles, a toothy kind of grin. Always
made me laugh when she smiled. You know how they say
redheads have a hot temper? That wasn't her at all. She was

easy going, so patient with me, always content to go with the flow. I didn't want a job that would take me away from her, I wanted stability, so I could be with her. That was our plan—together forever.

"After high school I found work around the harbour in St. John's and started working my way up, gaining experience. Trish always wanted to be a teacher, so I worked while she studied for her degree. We did it right, we played it smart. She finished her schooling and got a job at one of the primary schools in town. By then I was second mate on one of the ships, regular work, and we started to put aside a little money. We were twenty-four when we got married, but we had already been together eight years by then and Trish didn't want to wait to have kids. So, we started trying, and trying, and, it just wasn't happening. It went on like that for three, four years. Trish was going to doctors, getting hormone shots, nothing happened for a very long time. I would have been happy to drop it—I loved Trish, I spent my days out at sea, I didn't feel like my life was lacking. But she kept trying, you know? And she did get pregnant eventually. Man, I remember that day. She was so happy. When she miscarried a few weeks later… I never saw her like that. Not ever. I thought we were done with trying but no, she kept up with the hormone therapy and got pregnant again, then miscarried again. By the third, well, I finally sat her down and asked that we take a break from trying. We'd been married for five, maybe six years by then, and—it's not that I didn't want kids, if you can understand—I just wanted to enjoy our marriage while we were still young enough to enjoy it. She cried so much that day, we both did, but… Anyway, she agreed.

"A few years passed like that. Those were good years, really. I kept advancing, made it to first mate, then eventually captain. Trish absolutely loved being a teacher. In summer, when she was off work, she would tutor kids in math and science, anyone who needed it. I always felt grateful that she had found work that was meaningful to her. I mean, we had each other, and we had jobs that we loved. It's more than a lot of people have."

Mike stopped talking then. Chiara was still seated beside him and hadn't moved a muscle since he began. He appreciated that she was giving him the space he needed to tell his story. This was in fact the first time he'd done this since leaving St. John's four years earlier. Sure, there were people who knew the necessary bits, just enough not to pester him with questions. He had left St. John's to escape all the memories held by its hills and valleys, he'd had no desire to bring those memories with him, to share them with his new neighbours, to have them look at him the way others had looked at him. Telling Chiara though, it was different. It was necessary. He didn't know why but, he trusted her. He looked at her before continuing, giving her a faint hint of a smile. Chiara saw this, but his eyes were so sad that on instinct she picked up his hand and held it. She didn't speak though, not to interrupt him, and after several seconds of pause Mike spoke again.

"As it turned out, once we stopped trying so hard to have a baby, Trish fell pregnant. She didn't even tell me, not until she was almost three months along when it started to become obvious. She was worried she would miscarry and didn't want to put me through that again. But she didn't, and we had a beautiful, amazing baby boy. Connor. That was his name. He was so strong, and so smart. God, he was so smart. He had my looks but Trish's temperament, never put up too much of a fuss. We were so in love with him. And I would pinch myself, I didn't think it was possible to be that happy, to have that much love in one lifetime. I didn't take it for granted, no. I'm serious on that. I would have done anything for the two of them.

"Connor turned six in March. It had been a brutal winter and that month hadn't yet shown any signs of letting up. We had a small party at the house. My parents came over, some friends. We had a cake in the shape of a dinosaur, and we bought him this huge five hundred-piece block set. He couldn't wait for me to sit with him to construct that thing… We never did get to build it.

"A few days later, it was really snowy out. Rain and sleet and snow all mixed into one. There was also a bit of fog coming off the bay. Just a miserable day. I left early that morning. There was mechanical work being done on the fleet and I had a crew coming to the harbour to meet me. So I, uh, I'm not all that sure, but from what we could piece together, it seems that Trish was having car trouble that morning. She would have had to get to work, and Connor to school—they were at the same school of course. She never called me. That's the part that I always had trouble with. Maybe she didn't want to bother me? Knew I was busy that day? Maybe my parents happened to call, and it was just…fate? It might not have been any different, I know. I just—I just wish she would have called me. Wish I could have heard their voices that morning."

This time, when Mike paused, it was because the pain was too great. He let out a loud, open-mouthed sigh. Chiara could hear the pain in the words caught in his throat, the words he was finding the courage to say.

"So, um, St. John's is all winding roads, up and down hills. There's this one intersection—folks call it the 'Stop 'n Pray,' because you stop, and then you pray before you go again. Even on a good day it's hard to see when someone's coming, but that morning, like I said, it was terrible out. My dad was driving. My mom was in the passenger seat. Trish and Connor were in the back. There was this kid, sixteen years old and had just passed his driver's exam the week before. He had no place being out on the road that morning, his parents didn't even know that he'd borrowed the car. You know how you are at sixteen, you never think harm can come to you at that age. Or that you can bring harm to others. Anyway, witnesses say that Dad stopped the car at the stop sign, full stop, and waited a good amount of time to be sure the coast was clear. Dad wasn't one to take chances. But as he started to go this kid came flying over the hill, just way too fast. Surprised everyone, they said. But Dad's car was the only one in the intersection at the time. It was over before any of them could have done anything to stop it. Worst accident ever recorded in that spot. They..." Mike let out a single, strangled sob. "They were all gone. All of them. My wife, my child, my mum, my dad. My entire family. Even the kid. All of them. It took less than half a minute to destroy the life we had spent years building."

Looking Chiara in the eye once again he added, "It wasn't supposed to end like that. That wasn't supposed to be our story."

Chiara's eyes were red from the tears she was holding back, her heart ached for Mike and all that he'd lost. At a loss for words, she squeezed the hand she held between both of hers.

"The thing is," Mike said, "however I thought it was supposed to be, whatever I thought was supposed to happen, it's just not what happened. It took me a couple of years to get so far as accepting that, but even then... I've been dead inside. When I left St. John's, moved out here, it wasn't to start a new life. It never occurred to me that another life could exist outside of Trish and Connor. I just didn't want the reminders, I couldn't handle the memories. I could barely walk down the street without running into a colleague of my mom's or parents of Trish's students, or see Connor's friends playing at the park and knowing that he should've been there, playing with them. I was on a leave of absence from work, indefinitely, and I just couldn't bring myself to go back. I woke up one morning, got in my car and started driving. I wasn't thinking, I just drove. Somehow, I ended up in Queen's Cove. I saw the store and stopped in for some bottles of water and snacks. Burt was there, obviously, but so were Bill and Cheryl. I overheard them talking about a neighbour that had just passed away, and they mentioned that their house was on the market. It seemed fitting, you know? I jumped on it and never looked back. I hired a realtor to sell the two houses in the city, friends pitched in to help clear them out, but I've never been back."

He stopped talking then. Minutes passed, Mike watching the waves, Chiara watching Mike. She could see that his jaw was firmly set, that his brows were drawn together. She felt that he still had more to say but, couldn't imagine how there could possibly be more to his story. Mustering up the courage to speak she said, "Thank you, Mike. Thank you for telling me." Then, with a deep breath asked, "Why did you tell me?"

Mike hadn't moved, hadn't twitched. She wasn't even sure that he had heard her speak but, eventually, he did respond. "The thing is, that for the past four years I've been barely living. I go about my business—I've built a good little life here—but it's like I've been in limbo. No. Purgatory. Neither here nor there, not connected to anything or anyone. And it was okay, I didn't expect more nor was I looking for more. But then you came along and, I don't know what it is about you Chiara but, somehow you opened up my eyes a little, reminded me that there's still life to be lived. You weren't even trying, I know that. I can't even explain it. I'm forty-two years old though, and for the first time since the accident, I find myself wondering if I should be doing better than I have been, if I'm even doing right by my family to keep on as I've been. I hope that doesn't make you feel uncomfortable."

The look in his eyes as he said that was a combination of hope and anxiety, tinged with the sadness of all he had just shared. Chiara looked directly into his blue eyes and smiled softly.

"Uncomfortable? No, not at all. You've made me feel a lot of different things to be sure but, not uncomfortable. I want you to know, Mike, that you've been that person for me, too. I expected to come to Newfoundland and be alone, like I'm always alone, but then there was you. You reminded me that I can't keep trying to go through life alone. Mike, *you* can't keep going through life alone. I guess, maybe, we've been good for each other?" She said it as a question but they each took it as a statement, final. The words hung between them as they looked earnestly into each other's faces. The moment was heavy, and Chiara was eager to lighten the mood, for Mike's sake more than anything.

Without looking away, she reached back into her tote bag and, pulling out a smaller bag, held it up to Mike. "Marshmallow?"

Mike laughed with relief and grabbed the bag from her. "Yeah. Yeah...that sounds good."

They remained on the beach until the afternoon sun began to drop low in the sky. Once Mike had ripped off the band-aid, he found it became easier and easier to speak freely with Chiara about his life, and in a way, he felt lighter for it. For one thing, the proverbial elephant that had been parked between them all week was no longer there. Also, he found Chiara to be a good listener, and after so many years spent bottled up, a listening ear what just what he needed. For her part, Chiara enjoyed Mike's stories about his son, his family. She knew that she could never comprehend what Mike had been through, but there had been an entire life before that one fateful day that could not be ignored, and she didn't want either one of them to ignore it.

The mood between them was not exactly jovial, but it was no longer heavy, either. Comfortable. If either of them were to describe how they felt together that afternoon, roasting marshmallows, watching waves, putting logs on the flame, it would have come down to *comfortable*. Any awkwardness, tension or shyness between them had all but disappeared. At some point Chiara pulled the blanket from her bag and strung it over her lap, bringing her knees to her chest to snuggle in. Mike instinctively drew close beside her, pulling some of the blanket over his own lap, feeding her some of his warmth. When the temperature dipped further—once the fire had been extinguished and their things collected—Mike gave the blanket a quick shake and wrapped it closely around Chiara's shoulders, then took her by the arm and led her home.

Unlike the previous nights, neither of them were prepared to say good night at the base of the Boyd home stoop. It wasn't yet dark out, they still had time. Chiara didn't ask and Mike didn't offer, but they each agreed that Mike would follow her up the steps and inside.

"Hungry?"

He wasn't really but answered, "Peckish, a little."

"I'm not sure what I have to offer but let's take a look." Chiara led them both into the kitchen. As she bent to examine the contents of the fridge Mike looked to the corner, he had grown accustomed to checking the canvas for progress with each visit. This time, however, he found the painting turned around so that it was facing the wall. Disappointed, he questioned her about it.

"It's all done, finished it late last night." Seeing that Mike continued to look at the canvas, his interest obvious, made Chiara glad. Painting was such an important part of her life that Mike's curiosity and appreciation touched her heart in a way she hadn't experienced before. She found his opinion mattered to her, and yet, she understood instinctively that she'd already earned his respect. Still, she wasn't ready to share the finished product. Not yet. "No peeking!"

Mike stuck out his lower lip, feigning sadness, and she laughed.

"I'll show you eventually, just not yet. I'm still too close to it. I'd feel like I'm putting my heart on the table for you to examine."

"I feel like that's what I did this afternoon."

Chiara shut the fridge door and took a few steps in Mike's direction, searching for the appropriate response to Mike's statement, knowing that in fact he had indeed laid out the depths of his heart for her, and had trusted her in the process.

Mike, seeing in Chiara's face that she was searching for words, realized in that moment that what he wanted went beyond words. He took two great strides toward her, grabbing her around the small of her back with one hand, and with his second hand to her cheek he kissed her with the fervour of man whose need was deep.

Chiara had not been expecting a kiss, especially not after their conversation that afternoon, but she had been wanting it. Her back melted into Mike's hand, her own two hands held him on either side of his head, pulling him in closer, deeper. She could feel the heavy emotion behind his kiss, the longing, the need. She reciprocated by allowing her own need, her own longing, to be known and felt, and as such, they each worked to fill the other's void. Chiara wrapped a hand around the back of Mike's neck, the other against his back, and holding on tightly, pressed her body into his.

Mike's body responded in kind, he needed to feel every inch of her against him. Turning them slightly toward the table for support, Mike sought to explore Chiara's mouth with urgency and she readily accepted, inviting him to explore even further, adding more pressure to hold him to her.

With Chiara leaning against the table from behind and Mike leaning into Chiara, every kiss, every movement, brought with it the promise of a more intimate connection. It was impossible to escape their wanting, impossible to ignore the heat. Chiara's mind was fuzzy, she only knew what her body was telling her. As she felt Mike's body change against hers, she became filled with a burning sensation that began in her breasts and worked its way down. She pushed her body forward, he pushed back. The rocking sensation was driving her to delirium until finally she cried in desperation, "Mike!"

Mike heard his name on her lips and understood the intention. It took mere seconds before he entered her, at which point they both paused with a sigh before driving each other forward again. They were hot, frantic, and desperate. It had been years since either of them had experienced intimacy, each having gotten used to solitude in their own way. But this opportunity for togetherness, to drive a wedge between them and loneliness, brought out an urgent desire to satiate themselves and satisfy the other in the closest possible way.

It didn't take long. Chiara grabbed Mike's shoulders with both hands, shaking. Mike followed suit, unable to contain himself any longer. They leaned against each other for several minutes, hearts pounding loudly in their chests, their breathing fast and irregular.

Once he caught his breath, Mike carefully pulled away. He turned so that he was leaning against the table, side by side with Chiara. He looked sheepish as he sought the appropriate words to ensure that she was okay, that *they* were okay. "Well. That was...unexpected."

Chiara chuckled at the understatement, shaking her head. After a pause she turned toward Mike, eyebrow raised. "Want some eggs?"

"You have bologna!" Mike exclaimed, voice raised in sheer victory.

Chiara giggled as she responded. "Consider me converted." She was buttering toast and there were eggs scrambling on the stove. Mike had decided that he was hungry after all.

"Well you know you can't have eggs without bologna." He grabbed a pan and, cutting off two thick slices from the round of meat, set about frying them to add to their meal.

Once their food was plated, they turned to seat themselves at the table. Knowing that it would need to be addressed, Chiara decided to circle back to their earlier encounter. "You know, I'll never look at this table the same way again."

Mike nodded, the way he did when he was pretending to be serious. "Bill and Cheryl's imaginations couldn't handle it if they knew. Might need to keep this one between us."

"Indeed!" Changing her tone, she continued. "So…and don't get me wrong, I enjoyed everything that just happened, but…I want you to know that I understand. You know. We spent so much time talking about your wife down on the beach, I'm sure it brought up a lot of memories, and maybe you were feeling lonely…"

Mike put a hand over her wrist, resting it against the edge of her plate, fork in hand. He gave it a firm squeeze, making certain to establish eye contact before speaking. "You're right that this afternoon stirred up memories for me, and you're right that it was emotional. I have been in mourning for four years and it has been a lonely time. And I'll be honest with you, I'll always mourn them, all of them—they were all the family I've got. Or, had, anyway. But what happened here between us—actually, it was more like over here—" he winked at her while patting a spot on the hard wood tabletop, "that was just about you and me. I want you to know that. It's important to me that you know that."

A wave of relief swept through her, mind and soul. Chiara had given herself to Mike of her own accord. Her attraction to Mike had only increased with time, but so had her like of him. She really, really liked him. When it came down to it, her body had given itself over, without question, to the feelings she had cultivated for Mike in the short time she'd known him. She had been certain enough that the attraction was mutual, and in the heat of the moment that had been enough for her. However, while she had not felt bold enough to assume that he harboured any feelings for her, hearing in his voice that, maybe, possibly, he did…

"I'm very happy to hear that."

Mike smiled warmly. His blue eyes were soft as he regarded her, his grin crooked and adorable. "Trish and I met in high school. We started dating at sixteen. We were kids.

We grew up together, and as we grew our love for each other grew and matured and changed in many ways. It was special in its own way and I won't take away from that, but… Chiara, you have to know I'm developing feelings for you. It wasn't expected and it definitely wasn't planned—wasn't even wanted, until it happened. That day that we first met on the beach, something inside me just cracked right open at the sight of you. It scared me. I've never experienced that before, not as an adult. I just find that with every minute I spend near you, the clearer I am about wanting to know you."

"Mmm… That's funny."

"Funny?"

"Not funny *haha* but… The word *chiara*, translated it means *clear*."

"Hmm. Well. Appropriate, then, don't you think?"

Chiara smiled at him, this big, gentle man sitting before her in earnest. Two weeks ago, she would have sworn that such a man did not exist, someone who could occupy her mind in such a way. Two weeks ago, her life had felt hollow, but now there existed in Mike a hint, perhaps a promise, that she could one day have what her heart desired. Beyond the romantic feelings she was developing for him, she felt grateful to him for opening her up to the possibility. She understood that this was not some childhood crush or whirlwind vacation romance. What she felt about Mike had begun as a spark deep down in her gut, but that spark had ignited, and she had no desire to extinguish this flame.

Placing her fork down against the edge of her plate Chiara rose from her seat and leaned her body in Mike's direction. As she placed one hand down on his wide shoulder, he leaned back into his chair to make space for her. She looked him in the eyes for a good long time before lowering herself down onto his lap. Mike wrapped his arms around her waist in an easy embrace. Not breaking eye contact Chiara kissed him, a long, slow and languid kiss, invoking warm tingles in the back of his neck and down his spine. Mike succumbed to

Chiara's mouth, wordlessly giving her permission to do as she pleased and wordlessly Chiara took it. She covered his mouth fully with hers, bringing a moan to his lips before she slowed her pace again, leaving him wanting. Moving her lips across his face she kissed him gently on the forehead, and again on each temple before pressing down firmly once again, this time on his neck. Taking her time, she moved her lips from the base of one ear down to the hollow of his neck and back up. Although Mike was closely shaven, she could feel a small amount of stubble against her lips, his skin was rough as one who has spent much time out in the elements. He smelt good to her, distinctly masculine, fresh, natural. Working her way back up to his mouth she saw his eyes were closed, but he opened them again as he rolled his head upright, meeting her eyes evenly and without compunction. Giving him another strong, deep kiss before ending with a gentle tug on his lower lip, Chiara rested her forehead against his, noses touching, mouths mere inches apart.

She seemed to be considering something, but Mike remained wordless, enjoying the feel of her in his arms. Standing abruptly, Chiara walked backwards towards the hallway. "I'd like to go upstairs now." She turned and left the room, swaying her hips as she went. Seconds later he could hear her feet on the steps.

Mike leaned forward in his chair, his lips still wet from her kisses. With his hands to his knees he smiled with contentment. "Stay where you're to 'til I comes to where you're at, b'y." He spoke aloud but mostly to himself; he needed a second to regroup. Chiara was making him feel things, want things—he had no doubt that he would follow her up the stairs, but it had been so long since he had felt so alive, both physically and emotionally, that it was almost overwhelming. His mind felt thick, he wasn't operating on rational thought. For once, he realized, he liked it. Pausing a while longer as though to gather his strength, he pushed himself out of his chair and strode from the room.

"I'm coming b'y. I'm 'a comin'."

CHAPTER NINE

Chiara was splayed out on the sofa, sitting low against the edge of the bottom cushion rather than flat against its back, her arms loosely down by her sides, her legs hanging purposeless over the sofa's edge. It was only once she sat down that she realized how tired she was and closed her eyes to feel the sweet relief of rest. She was tired, but she was happy, and relaxing by herself on the sofa she allowed her body to give way to the full effects of her contentment. A warm, fuzzy feeling had started at the base of her neck and was spreading like a star, outward in all directions. It eased across her shoulders, releasing any tension being held there, and the tingling continued down her back and up, reaching high around her head like fingers through her hair. It was a pleasurable sensation and she relished it, a small smile sitting idly on her lips.

She heard footsteps down the hall and opened her eyes in time to see Mike enter the living room carrying two mismatched mugs of steaming coffee. Her smile widened as she raised herself higher on the sofa, as much at the sight of the coffee as who was carrying it.

"You're a lifesaver," she said to him as he set the mug down on the coffee table. She picked it up between her two hands, inhaling its robust scent before taking her first sip. It was hot, comforting, and just what she needed in her fatigued state. "Mmmmmmm."

Mike sat on the cushion beside her, taking a similar stance, and sipped from his own mug. "Yep. I agree."

She laughed. "I think I'm getting too old for nights like that."

"Yeah, me too. Was fun though."

She eyed him as he sat beside her, utterly relaxed. Wearing only his t-shirt and boxers, he seemed unbothered by the morning chill. This only made Chiara snuggle deeper into her pajamas. She eyed the blanket that was strewn across the *La-Z-Boy*, wondering if it was worth getting up to retrieve it. Mike was looking at her though, and she became distracted by his smile.

Their night together had been long, slow, serene and sensual. There had been periods of intimacy followed by periods of quiet conversation, whispering to each other in the dark of night, allowing their fingers to stroke and wander, eventually leading to intimacy once again. There had been very little sleep, and at the first hints of pink streaking across the early morning sky they had given up on the idea altogether. They had made their way back downstairs just before seven in the morning, groggy, elated, and a little disoriented. Chiara could barely register what day it was, what her plans were for that day, or how she intended on doing said plans. All she knew for certain was the sofa, that coffee, and Mike, solidly and comfortably beside her. She looked at the hand closest to her, hanging casually against his leg, and recalled the feel of it against her skin. Instantly she felt something give rise within her, surprising her, as she thought she'd been sufficiently satiated. But there it was, the magnetic effect Mike had on her. She sighed, gave his hand an affectionate rub, and turned back to her coffee. She was much too tired.

"It was fun, definitely. Too much fun. I can't believe I have to leave in a couple of days, I feel like we've only just gotten started." She saw a shadow move across Mike's face at the mention of her leaving. This surprised her. They both knew that her time was limited. She was on vacation, it was not as though this had been a permanent move. The thought of leaving did cause her chest to constrict, however, and by the expression on Mike's face it was obvious that he was having a similar reaction. "I mean, the Boyds did say they'd be gone all summer. I suppose I could always write to them, ask if I can stay on longer?" She allowed this suggestion to hang between them, fully expecting that Mike would jump on the idea and that a decision would be solidified. His response, however, was inexplicably cool.

"Yeah, well, I guess that's a possibility." His body had tensed, rather than relaxed he was suddenly terse.

After the deep bonding of their all-night exchange Chiara was confused and put off, as much by the lack of enthusiasm in his response as by the total change of attitude. Unsure what to say or how to respond she chose not to say anything. This silence between them expanded, both of them feeling the weight of its strain.

Mike drained his coffee and sat up. "Can I get you a refill?"

"No, thanks… I'm still nursing this one."

He nodded, slowly. His eyes darted around the room, as though he had been relying on the coffee as a reason to excuse himself and was now searching for an alternative. Not finding one, however, he altered his course.

"Well, I guess I should probably get home, get showered. It looks like it should be a beautiful day, I'm sure I can get a fair amount of work done if I hop to it." He looked at Chiara from the corner of his eye, hesitant, then slapped his hands to his knees with resolve as he stood up.

Chiara watched as he headed up the stairs to grab the remainder of his clothes. She was confused, not understanding of what was currently happening. Minutes ago, they were at ease, contented and in harmony. Something between them had changed very suddenly and, being unable to pinpoint the cause was adding to her confusion.

Mike bounded back down the stairs mere seconds later. "I'll…uhh... I'll see you later?"

Still on the sofa but no longer laid back, Chiara could only manage to utter a one-word response. "Sure." It sounded passive-aggressive, even to her. She had not intended it to be, however satisfied herself in acknowledging that that it was at least an appropriate occasion for the tone. As the door shut behind Mike her tone changed to one of confounded disappointment.

"What in the actual heck just happened?" she asked to an empty room.

———————

As Mike returned home, he was wracked with guilt. Pushing his way inside he paced the front room, mind spinning. He knew exactly what had just happened. Chiara had reminded him that her time in Came to Stay was finite, and he panicked.

Their night together had been amazing—the entire day had been. Since opening up to Chiara down at the beach he'd felt lighter, and also grounded. Surer of himself and his own emotions than he had been in a while. Chiara had opened him up, and once open he had greedily accepted all she had to offer. But now, faced with her imminent departure, his instinct was to protect himself before he went in too deep.

She had offered to extend her stay—Bill and Cheryl would have readily accepted, and with a career like Chiara's she had the flexibility to stay on longer, perhaps even for the entire summer. That would be fun. That would be wonderful, he admitted to himself. But then what? She was from away. At some point she would need to return home, and he would need to stay here, in Newfoundland. It's where he belonged. Letting her go after two weeks together hurt, he couldn't imagine what it would feel like to let her go after two months.

He'd already loved and lost once in his life, he couldn't allow himself to go down that road again. His heart couldn't bear it.

No, it would be easier if she just left as scheduled. Simpler for them both. They would at least have the memory of their one incredible night together, their one, unbelievable night...

Holy hell. What am I doing? Mike continued to pace the room, running a hand through his disheveled waves. *I don't want her to leave...* He felt a tightness in his chest at the very idea. His mind, though, was racing ahead. He had loved once, and it seemed to him by this point in his life that you couldn't have love without loss eventually following behind. He didn't think he could take it.

Mike glanced up and his eyes fell upon the portrait. Crossing the room, he lifted it off the wall, staring at the faces as he dropped down into the seat nearest him. His thumb brushed against the faces as his eyes moved about the frame—his beloved mum, his steadfast dad, his darling wife whom he had promised to be with forever, and his child, his heart, the greatest gift ever given to him, then taken away.

His eyes welled up as he took in the minute details of his son's picture, the colour of his hair, the shape of his face, the small scar near his left temple from when he had scratched himself on a piece of wood at a playground when he was just three years old. Trish had told Connor that the scar was shaped like a fishing rod, and that it meant he would grow up to love the sea as much as his dad, turning his injury into something that Connor was proud of.

Trish. His Trish. His wife. His love. He'd never even had the chance to say a proper goodbye. The last time he'd seen her alive she was still in bed; he hadn't wanted to disturb her. Passing his fingers over her photographed face the tears grew heavy, sliding down his face and dropping with dense plops onto the glass of the frame.

Here he was, agonizing over his deepening feelings for the woman sitting in the house with the green roof next door, while the memory of his dead wife still hung over him every minute of every day. He needed to resolve his feelings, and he could think of only one way to do it.

Putting the portrait down on the seat beside him he paused a few seconds as though questioning his resolve, but having made up his mind he rose up, grabbed his car keys and headed out.

––––––––––––

Chiara heard the car rev up and drive off. She didn't bother to get up, just to watch the car as it drove away down the lane. She knew it was Mike, leaving again. A wave of disappointment rushed through her. Disappointment in Mike for running away from his problems, and disappointment in herself for developing feelings for a man who was obviously emotionally incapable of feeling the same way about her.

She raised both hands and worked them into fists, shaking them in the air. "Argh! What is it with me? I'm just not meant for love." The tears came fast and without warning. Her face began to twitch, her eyes to blink quickly, as she tried without success to hold them at bay. Before she knew it, she was sobbing loudly, feeling the sobs come up from her very core, working their way up her chest and throat before escaping painfully into the open air. Her shoulders heaved, her nose ran down in streams, blending with the gush of tears.

Bringing her fists down she slammed them into her thighs, willing herself to stop crying yet physically and emotionally incapable of controlling the flow. The truth was that she had wanted things to work out with Mike. The truth was that last night had opened something in her that she hadn't known existed, a feeling she had never felt before, a feeling she was now grasping to keep hold of. The truth was that she was falling in love, and now Mike was gone. The last time he ran off it had been for days. She knew it was completely within the realm of possibility that he would stay away until she was gone for good.

It was ironic, really. She had come out here to clear her head and reassess, so she could move on with her life as an independent professional. She had instead allowed herself to fall in love, the one thing she was certain would never happen. But she would leave Newfoundland just as alone as she had arrived.

———————

The three-hour drive to St. John's had done nothing to clear Mike's thoughts, but his resolve over what he needed to do had only strengthened. He took a deep breath as he pulled up to the cemetery gates, then slowly eased the car through and down its winding pathways. It had been four years since Mike was last here, four long years spent intentionally staying away. He didn't have much confidence in his ability to see this through gracefully, but he was determined to see it through, nonetheless. He drove as far as he could, then walked the remainder of the way to the burial plots. They were together, all of them. His mum and dad shared one headstone, his wife and son shared another. Mike had purchased one additional plot for himself—certain as he was four year ago that he would follow his family to the ground. He sat cross-legged on the empty plot and regarded what was left of the family he once cherished.

Thirty minutes later he was still sitting in the same position, having lost all sense of time. Shaking himself forcibly, he rose to stand before each grave individually. He read their names aloud, touching each stone as he did, feeling the hard coldness beneath his fingers. Emotional, he knelt to clear away the weeds and debris that had accumulated over time. Mike silently chastised himself briefly for delaying the inevitable, but ultimately these were not delay tactics. Mike was mourning, with the intention of moving on.

Time continued to move slowly as he agonized over the words caught in a lump in his throat. Mike was pacing back and forth before the stones, eyeing the leaves, the trees, the blades of grass. He rubbed his face in his hands over and over as he searched for the courage he needed to continue. Dropping, finally, to his knees before Trish and Connor's grave, he began to cry for the second time that day.

"Oh, guys—Oh, guys... It has been so, so hard without you here. I've missed you so much, I've been dead inside without you both. These past four years, honestly, I've been barely living. Not a day goes by without some random memory popping into my mind, where I don't think of you while I'm cooking dinner or smelling you when I go to sleep or hearing your voices while I'm driving my car... Y'know, people would tell me that I needed to move on but, I didn't want to. Move on from what? I'd say. I preferred to torture myself, because at least it kept you guys close. The thing is... The thing is—Okay, here's the thing. I've met someone. Only recently, mind you, but it's been enough to show me, to teach me, that I can't just let myself die. That I need to keep on living. I need to learn how to live this life without you guys in it. And not just that, I need to remember what love is, too. I can't keep going as I've been going. And I feel so guilty. Guys, I feel so guilty. But I'm here to ask you to forgive me. I'm here to ask your permission. I'm here to let you know that I'm ready to live again, and that I need to move on. I won't forget you, please don't ever think that I would forget you. You're irreplaceable, you know that. But there is an alternate life available to me, one that will make me happy. And I just hope that you're okay with it. I hope that you can accept it. I really hope that you can forgive me. I need to do this. I have to do this."

Mike stopped to run the back of his hand under his sniffling nose. He let out an audible sigh and waited for the next wave of words to come forth. He felt like he was choking on a multitude of emotions but primarily on an overwhelming sense of guilt. Together forever, that had been his promise. Here he was asking for the permission to break it.

A bird was cawing overhead, loudly enough to catch Mike's attention, albeit distractedly. He watched through tear-ridden eyes as two black crows circled overhead, cawing in time with each other. Mike watched them with disinterest at first, caught up as he was in his own thoughts. Their presence, however, was forceful, loud as they were, and it became impossible not to give them his full attention. He watched them as they flew to the branch of a tall maple nearby, sitting side by side. He felt as though they were looking directly down at him and his breath caught in his throat. Being a man of the sea and a Newfoundlander to the core, he never spurned superstition and folklore, so he knew, of course, that two black crows flying overhead was a symbol of good luck. And these two crows were certainly seeking his audience. He glanced at the names on the stone and back up at the crows. They cawed again in unison then flew up, circling the sky above him two more times before flying gracefully away.

Mike closed his eyes and bowed his head as though in prayer. When he raised it again, he felt lighter and an expression of gratitude spread across this face.

"Thank you, both of you. Thank you."

Two hours after she'd heard Mike's car drive off down the lane, Chiara was all cried out and was self-medicating with sun and sand down by the beach. She was sitting on her favourite rock, watching the ocean as she had so many times over these past two weeks. She had allowed herself her moments of self-pity, but she had also been raised to keep her chin up, and years of independence had taught her the value of stubbornness and strength. She would be fine. She was resolved to be fine.

She had already admitted to herself her feelings for Mike so ignoring the love she felt or denying it wasn't an option. However, if there was one thing Chiara knew it was how to live alone. Going back to that would bring no great change in her life.

She was clinging to this knowledge when she felt her cell phone vibrating in her pants pocket. Tempted to ignore it at first, she wondered suddenly if it was Mike. She was frustrated at her eagerness as she checked the call display, but also frustrated at her disappointment when she saw her mom's number flash across the screen. She couldn't allow herself to continue on in this way. Unintentionally, Chiara was hardening her heart, protecting it from further pain. Intentionally, she was making plans to return to Montreal to continue her single life with gusto.

Distractedly, she answered the phone. "Hi, Ma."

The sounds coming through the line were garbled and it took Chiara a few seconds to realize that her mom was crying. "Ma? Ma, what's wrong? Is it Nonna?"

"Chiara, sweetheart. It's your dad."

Several hours after speaking with her mom Chiara was pacing the house from room to room. She had raced up to the house after speaking with her mom, expecting to pack up and leave as quickly as possible. However, a phone call to the airline slowed her down. The soonest she could reschedule her flight was for seven that evening. Chiara had mindlessly set about packing her things and putting the home back in order. She washed dishes and towels, swept floors and watered plants. She cleaned every surface she had touched. Her mind was numb, as was her entire body. She had cried so much that morning, cried in her own well of self-pity, that now when she needed tears for someone else there were none left. Instead, she worked to keep herself busy as the time passed with excruciating slowness.

Finally determining that it was time to leave she walked to the kitchen to retrieve her last remaining parcel, her other bags being already packed into the car. In the living room she grabbed her purse from the sofa and the house key from a shelf on the wall, then left the house for good, returning the key to its hiding spot under the bench before heading downstairs. Rather than going directly to her rental car she walked over to Mike's house, her feet feeling heavy every step of the way.

She had told Mike that her painting of Came to Stay would remain in Came to Stay and she'd meant it. Despite their abrupt and confusing ending, Chiara had cherished the time she spent with Mike immensely, and she was grateful to him, also, for teaching her something about herself that she wouldn't have learned had they never met. She was capable of love and deserved to receive it. It hurt, now, but the lesson was worth it. Leaning the painting gently against the outer wall she allowed her fingers to linger on it momentarily. She had wrapped it in some Christmas paper she had found in an upstairs closet, causing it to look out of place on the sunny porch. She debated briefly, then quickly pulled a notebook and pen from her purse. Tearing out a page she scrawled across it: *For you, with thanks. Chiara.* Folding the note over the painting's edge there was nothing left to do but go home.

———————

Mike was only about a half hour from Came to Stay. Anxious as he was to see Chiara, to set things right with a free conscience and open heart, there were also practical concerns to contend with. A round trip to St. John's meant that his car needed gas, and he was coming up on the only gas station in a forty kilometre radius.

He had a vision replaying in his mind, of pulling up in front of their homes, bounding up the steps and pounding on the door until Chiara agreed to speak with him. Knowing that he had behaved badly that morning, he fully intended to plead for her to stay on longer.

Feeling annoyed at the delay as he pulled into the gas station, he issued himself a warning. *Be quick about it, MacCloud, you've got business to attend to.*

———————

As Chiara pulled out onto the main highway that would eventually carry her all the way to St. John's, she noticed the sign for the gas station in the distance. On reflex she glanced to her gas gauge. In truth she had barely driven the car during her time in Came to Stay. Easing her foot off the gas she debated. On the one hand she would need to put gas in the car before returning the rental vehicle, but on the other, she just wanted to get moving, to narrow the distance between her and her dad. Filling up near the airport made more sense anyway. Pressing harder on the gas pedal she set her eyes forward, intent now on leaving Newfoundland for good.

———————

There were two things that Mike noticed, simultaneously, as he pulled his car into the driveway: Chiara's car was gone, and there was a parcel by his front door. He understood their meaning immediately and banged a hand against the steering wheel in frustration. In wanting to avoid the prospect of another love lost, he had succeeded in doing just that. He had messed up, he knew that. He didn't know whether it could be fixed.

"Well, this is a fine kettle of fish you got yourself into, isn't it?"

He went immediately to the painting, carrying it inside before unwrapping it delicately from its decorative paper. The finished product was more beautiful than he could ever have imagined. As beautiful to him as its creator. He didn't know what had enticed Chiara to gift it to him, he definitely didn't feel as though he deserved it. But as much as it reminded him that he was now alone, again, it was also a breathtaking souvenir of an incredible period of time. He would always be grateful to Chiara for this painting. He would always be grateful to Chiara, period.

CHAPTER TEN

Paul knocked hard on the front door of Chiara's condo.

It had been a month since he had last seen her at her father's funeral, and just as much time since they'd last spoken. Paul had sent her several messages since that day—at first a few words to let her know he was thinking of her, then questions to be sure she was okay, and finally, more frantic messages, imploring her to respond. She hadn't, and he was worried about his friend.

"Chiara! Open the door. Chiara it's me!"

Three or four minutes passed as Paul continued to knock and call out—long enough for passersby to look up from the sidewalk and take notice—before hearing the clicking noise of the door being unlocked from the inside. When the door finally opened, he was taken aback.

Chiara looked pale, almost sickly. Her long curls were up in a careless bun atop her head, she was wearing pajamas that looked like they were in need of a change, and the pallor of her skin was a far cry from its usual healthy olive glow, especially at this time of year when she would normally be spending copious hours outdoors in her garden. Paul grimaced. He wasn't pleased with finding her in this way.

"Well, aren't you a sight for sore eyes!" It was meant to be sardonic—expecting, as was their practice, a witty retort in return—but Chiara didn't appear to notice.

"Hey. Come on in." She turned abruptly and walked away, leaving him on the landing with the door wide open. He let out a slow breath as he watched her. This was not good.

Paul found her in the bedroom she used as her studio, sitting cross-legged on the floor in front of a medium-sized canvas. He stopped in his tracks as he entered the room, however, shocked for the second time this visit by the scene before him.

"What the…?"

Paul began to walk, very slowly, about the room. In all their years of friendship Paul had only been in her studio a handful of times but, he knew this was different. Chiara's creative process was usually calm and methodical. She was a dreamer but also a planner. But this—this was pure, raw creation. The room was filled with canvases propped up against walls and each other. The canvases all depicted the same beach scene, but from different angles and perspectives. The style was more loose, more painterly, than Chiara's typical controlled brush strokes, and this also made them more evocative. They were good. Damn good. Paul assumed this burst of creative genius had spun from the death of Chiara's father, but the curator in him couldn't help but be excited by this artistic cornucopia.

"So," he began, "not much going on around here, I see." He was working hard to get a reaction out of her and was rewarded with a small smirk.

"No, not much at all." Chiara was blunt, she sounded tired, but she wasn't unhappy to see Paul, either. Her mind was in a fog. She had barely communicated with anyone, aside from her mother and grandmother, over the past month, and had even fewer instances of leaving the confines of her condo. It took effort but she managed to shut her mind to the solitary thoughts she'd become used to entertaining and turned her attention on her guest. "I'm sorry. I'm being rude. Would you like some tea?"

Paul followed her into the kitchen. "You know you look terrible, right?"

"Gee, thanks."

"It's not that I don't love you still, but it would be nice to see you in some clean clothes."

Chiara's instinct was to make a sarcastic retort but, she knew that he was right. She opted instead for the truth. "I just haven't been feeling well lately."

Paul assumed, once again, that she was referring to her father so decided to change the subject. "Tell me about this beach. It's obviously meaningful to you."

Chiara sighed. "It is…in many ways. For one, it's where I was sitting when my mom called me about Dad—"

"Oh, I'm sorry! Here I was trying to change the subject!"

"No, no. It's okay. Really. Listen, I'm forever grateful that I got back to Montreal before he passed away. I would never have forgiven myself if I hadn't had a chance to say goodbye. I'm still mad at him for letting me go in the first place, for keeping his illness secret. I'm mad that I didn't spend his last few weeks with him, so it's true, there is pain associated with the beach. But there's also joy. My first time ever falling in love with someone, in all of my adult life, happened on that beach. I lost that too—and I'm…I'm terribly sad about that, but it's a beautiful memory that I hold dear. Love and loss, right? That beach is the bearer of my heart."

"That's so poetic."

"*Shut up.*"

Paul chuckled. "Hurry up with that tea. Now that you've let out that juicy tidbit I'm not leaving here until I hear all."

"So that's about it," Chiara concluded. "That's the whole story."

"And you haven't spoken with him since? I mean, you didn't even reach out to let him know why you left so abruptly?"

"Well... To be fair, he left abruptly first."

"Yeah, but—Chiara, you don't know what was going through his mind. You have no idea why he took off, same as he has no idea about you. For all you know, he could have gotten a call about a house on fire, or...or, someone got into an accident with a moose! The point is that you made an assumption, but you don't actually know why he left. This is all just too tragic. My sensibilities are too weak to handle it!"

Chiara couldn't tell whether Paul was squealing or whining, but either way she appreciated his melodrama. After a month of relative solitude this interaction was working to bring her out of her shell. "So, what would you have me do? Call him up after a month and say, 'Hey, Mike, whadda ya at?'"

Paul gave her a blank stare.

"It's Newfoundland speak. Never mind, you get my drift."

"You could go back out there. I know that Bill is still away, the house is still empty."

"Oh, no. No. No, I can't do that. Imagine he returned home that day to find me gone and felt *relief.* That would just be awkward. And stalkerish. Plus, I have Ma to think about now. It's just her and Nonna, they need me right now."

"Because you've been doing so much for them, holed up in your condo all month? Come on! This is like the plot line of a bad romance movie. Don't be a bad romance movie."

"Paul, listen to me. I cannot just roll up to Came to Stay with a smile on my face and pretend that there's nothing else going on." Chiara turned serious then, her tone descended a notch and she was looking down at her hands, wrapped around the delicate teacup, as she spoke. "If anything, there's too much at stake."

Paul was silent for a while, something entirely uncharacteristic of him but necessary as he sought a solution for his friend. He looked up suddenly, with an air of determination. "Fine, then. I know what I need to do."

"What's that?"

"Lead the horse to water. What happens after that is up to you."

———————

Mike was balancing on the edge of a wood support beam. He was simultaneously annoyed with the slow progress on the porch construction and, pleased at how it was now coming along. During Chiara's visit work had practically come to a halt, and after she disappeared so suddenly, it had taken a few weeks for his motivation to return. Realizing one day that he could benefit from the distraction, he'd set to work.

The dry rot had been more extensive than he first realized. Before he knew it, the entire porch had been demolished and he was reconstructing it one new cedar beam at a time. There was something wholly satisfying about this kind of work, and seeing the porch come together brought Mike a deep sense of gratification.

It was a beautiful June day. The air was fresh from the breeze drifting inland off the sea. It was the perfect day for a walk along the shoreline and on reflex he looked over to the house next door, his heart suddenly heavy. Mike had not been to the beach since the day he and Chiara had eaten hot dogs and marshmallows before a lingering bonfire, the day he'd opened up to her. The day he had admitted to himself that he was in love. He couldn't return now, the memory was still too raw and the pain too present. He guided his mind back to the job at hand, imploring himself to remain focused.

His phone began to vibrate unexpectedly from his back pocket. Mike paused, seriously considering ignoring it altogether, but politeness got the better of him and he pulled out the phone.

"Hello?"

"Hallo Mike, it's Ted. Wonderin' if ye could spare me a few hours t'morrow mornin'. I have some things I'd like to discuss."

Mike looked forlornly at his toolbox, he wasn't willing to put a pause on the progress he was making. Still, he knew why Ted was calling and decided it was prudent to have that conversation.

"You bet, Skipper. I'll be there first thing."

Ted prepared mugs of tea for the three men and carried them over to the small table in the bridge of his fishing vessel. "Here ya go, boys."

Mike and Ron accepted the mugs gratefully. "Thanks, Skipper," they said in unison.

Ted seated himself and began. "Mike, ye might be wonderin' why I called ya here this mornin'. I have a business proposition for ya and I'm hopin' ye'll be interested."

Mike listened as Ted laid out his plans to purchase more boats, expanding the fleet and the business at the same time.

"I know it's late in the season for this year but I wanted to get the ball rollin' so we can be ready for next season. Whadda ya think?"

Mike sat, looking pensively into his mug of orange pekoe. What *did* he think? That was a good question. On the one hand, he had a great respect for Ted, and knew he would make for an ideal business partner. And Mike did have the money. The idea of running a rig again, of being on the water full time, called to him in a way it hadn't in years. He truly missed the sea. But on the other hand, was this how he wanted to do it?

He thought about his family. This was their money he'd be investing after all—his inheritance, the capital from the sale of their city homes, and Trish's life insurance policy—and he wondered if this was how they would choose to spend it and, also, whether it was something they would be proud of. He considered the lifestyle of a full-time fisherman, too. It was a far cry from four years of relative unemployment. He was no stranger to hard work, but he did need to be certain that this was a change in the right direction.

The last time he had been on a boat was with Chiara, the day he took her on a whale watching tour for her birthday. Something clicked within him, like the snap of a finger or flash of light. Instantly he knew what he wanted to do.

———————

"Cobalt Door Gallery, can I help you?"

"Hi there. Yes. I'm wondering if I can speak to the gallery manager or curator please."

Paul had formulated his plan and was putting it into action. He didn't exactly have Chiara's consent, but to him that was a minor detail. He didn't want to bother her too much while she was still in mourning, anyway.

A friendly woman named Joanne took the phone and Paul started in on his pitch. He explained that he ran a gallery in Montreal, and that one of his prize artists had recently returned from an extended stay in the Bonavista Peninsula. He emphasized that she had been so inspired by the natural beauty of the countryside—intentionally laying on the praise as thick as he could, hoping it would bring out her pride in her home and native land—and that she had been painting up a storm since her return to Montreal.

"Now I *could* show these here in my own gallery, but I thought, how delightful would it be if her vernissage took place in Newfoundland itself. Being, obviously, the root of her inspiration."

"Verni-what?"

"Vernissage. Is that not the word you use? An exhibition opening? A soirée on behalf of the artist and her work?"

"Oh, I see!" Joanne had remained silent through much of Paul's sales pitch, but not due to lack of interest. She had quickly searched the name Chiara Costa online and had been browsing the artist's website during their call. She liked what she saw very much, and by the time it was her turn to speak she was itching with excitement. "Yes, I think that is a lovely idea. What did you have in mind?"

Paul went into further details about the work itself, the number of paintings he could offer and relative sizes, and expectations surrounding compensation for Chiara. For her part, Joanne took notes and promised to contact Paul once she had a chance to assess possible layouts for the exhibition. Most of their business concluded, Paul ventured forward with a few additional requests.

"Two more things, Joanne, if you don't mind."

"Of course."

"First, when the time comes, I just thought, and this is just an idea, that perhaps the show could be advertised in the local papers up in Bonavista—I assume there is a local paper up there?"

"I couldn't say for certain, but, yes, there must be. Plus, I do know that the paper here in St. John's does get up there with the weekend edition, so between the two there could be some exposure."

"Joanne, you read my mind. I just thought, you know, since that area is the basis of these works that it might be interesting for some of the residents."

"Consider it done, we'll be sure to bring in some media coverage."

"Wonderful! And lastly—I'm crossing my fingers that this doesn't present any scheduling conflicts for you—it is imperative that the show takes place by the fall at the latest. It can't go into winter, it can't wait until next year."

"Okay... You understand that we don't normally operate this way?"

"I do! Joanne, I do. If someone tried to dictate the schedule at my gallery, I'd tell them to take a hike. There are...special circumstances behind my request. I understand that this may not work for you, but I'm crossing fingers over here that it does." Paul was laying it on thick and was counting on the kindness of the Newfoundland people to carry him the rest of the way. He wasn't above playing the dead father card—reserving it for an emergency play—but as it turned out it wasn't necessary.

"Well, you're in luck, Paul. We had a cancellation in October, and I haven't filled that window. It's yours if you want it."

She didn't know it but as the words left her mouth, Paul began to dance about his office. "Joanne, I could kiss you!"

"Hello?"

"Finn? It's Mike. I was thinking about taking a drive up to Trinity this week. Any chance you're free to meet up for a beer?"

Chiara pulled up to her mom's house in Montreal-East. It was a small home attached on both sides, one of four in a solid row. The street was lined with identical quadruplexes, all with the same aluminum garage doors and slanting driveways.

Nonna had moved in with her daughter-in-law after the funeral. Neither of them cared to be alone, each of them seemed to have aged years in a very short period of time. When altogether, they were three generations of strong, independent women, grieving for the one man they all mutually adored. There were nights when Chiara preferred not to visit, the air in the home hanging heavily about the senior women. Yet, she couldn't stay away, either. *Misery loves company, et cetera, et cetera*, she thought to herself as she opened the front door and stepped into the foyer.

Chiara hoped that her presence tonight would be different. She hoped that she would help to lift their spirits. She sighed, deeply. *They'll either be happy, or, they'll feel much, much worse.* She wasn't sure which.

Her mom had heard the door open and came immediately to greet Chiara. "Hi, *bella*. I'm so happy to see you."

"Hi, Ma. Is Nonna here? I have something I wanted to talk with you guys about."

CHAPER ELEVEN

Patty was sitting on her stool behind the bakery counter, reading the newspaper half-heartedly as she waited for her scones to finish baking. She gave the air a sniff—*Nope, not yet!*—and turned to a new page.

The store was quiet. Kids were back in school and families were returning to routine after the free-for-all that is summer vacation. Construction workers were working longer hours to complete their projects before the first frost, and the fishermen were doing their best to make the most of their end of season. At two o'clock on a Tuesday afternoon, it was just her and Burt in the store, and—given that Burt was currently napping on a lounge chair in the supply room—she couldn't exactly take his presence into account. She was alone and bored for it. The stagnation was causing her humour to wilt.

She turned the page again, allowing her eyes to scan the page, stopping quite suddenly as they caught sight of something familiar. Patty blinked rapidly as though to wake up her brain, then read the advertisement again.

"Oh, sweet baby Jesus! Oh my, oh my, oh… Where is that Burt when I need him? Argh!" She rasped her knuckles against the counter, followed by wringing her hands together, then thumped them both down quickly and loudly onto the counter. *What* is *a woman to do?*

She heard a car door bang shut outside and shook her head with annoyance. *Not now!* But her annoyance quickly dissolved as the bell above the door chimed, followed by Mike's smiling face as he entered.

"Aren't you a sight for sore eyes!"

"And that's exactly why I drive the extra twenty minutes in the wrong direction to shop here, Patty." Mike widened his smile for Patty's benefit.

"Ye'll be returning from Trinity again, then?"

"You bet. I just need to pick up a few things for dinner and then I'm heading straight home. I'm beat!"

"I'm sure! You've been working so hard lately!"

"Yeah, but, it's all worth it in the long run. Hey—what's that I'm smelling?"

"Oh, mercy me, I forgot all about my scones! You wait here, I'll pack some up for you." Rather than hopping immediately off her stool, however, Patty took a few extra seconds to fold her newspaper, leaving the page she had been reading exposed, then folded it in half from there, and folded it once more until it was a quarter of its original size. She placed the newspaper at the edge of the counter furthest from her, text turned so that she was reading it upside down. The truth was that she did not trust the male gender to connect the dots when there were dots to be connected, and if it wasn't for the scent of the scones warning her to remove them from the oven immediately or bear the consequences of a burnt batch, she likely would have taken a yellow highlighter and traced a square around the advertisement.

As it was, Mike would not have taken notice of the newspaper were it not for Patty's theatrics. He was tired and hungry. Also, he generally reserved himself for the weekend edition, preferring to take his news in a leisurely manner. But he knew Patty well enough to know when she wanted him to pay attention, and as she placed the paper firmly on the counter, looking him meaningfully in the eye before heading for the kitchen, he knew this was one of those times.

With trepidation he headed for the counter, approaching the paper as though it were contaminated. He looked down at the text out of the corner of one eye at first, then, his eyes widening, he picked up the folded paper, holding it close for a better read.

"Sweet baby Jesus."

Patty, spying from the doorway to ensure that her plan had been successful, nodded to herself with satisfaction. *Mission accomplished, if I do say so myself. So long as he doesn't do anything daft, all will be well.* Her eyes narrowed then as she looked Mike up and down, wondering whether she could trust him not to be daft. Undecided, she stepped out from the kitchen.

"Here y'are, love. Fresh from the oven."

Mike was visibly distracted but came to his senses at the sound of Patty's voice. Placing the newspaper back down on the counter he struggled to speak. "Thanks, Patty. I, uh…I'll just grab a steak and be going. Why don't you ring those up for me?"

Patty was already putting a cardboard box filled with a half-dozen scones into a paper bag. "Don't be silly, these are on the house."

"Keep that up, Patty, and you'll go out of business."

"Bah," she said, waving the idea away with her hand, "nonsense. Besides, quiet as it is here today these'll just go to waste. Everyone knows that when it comes to scones, you have to dig right in, or they'll go stale." Looking Mike directly in the eye, she added the newspaper to the bag. "Here, take this as well. I'm done with it."

Mike paid for his steak and was heading for the door just as Burt stepped out from the back room, disheveled from his nap. Mike turned back before opening the door, giving a nod to Burt before settling his gaze on Patty.

"Thank you, Patty."

Patty returned his gaze meaningfully. "My pleasure, love.

My pleasure."

As Mike left, Burt turned to Patty with questioning eyes. "What was that all about now?" He was rubbing the sleep from his face and Patty smiled. She gave him a pat on the arm before turning away.

"Just some scones, love. Freshly baked."

The doorbell rang, causing Chiara to pause with her knife in the air mid-chop. It was early afternoon and she was starving. She had worked through the morning, finding her groove and not wanting to let up until she finished what she had started, but her stomach was now growling angrily as a result. She was debating over whether or not to answer the bell—she wasn't expecting anyone and, assuming it was a delivery, decided they could just leave the package by the door—but as the bell rang insistently for a second time, her curiosity got the better of her.

As she moved toward the door, she unconsciously patted the messy mass of her clipped-up hair, suddenly aware that she was still wearing pajamas. Undeterred, however, she opened the door to find a tall, well-dressed man standing on the landing. She could see through the fitted slacks and polo he wore that he was lean and sculpted, the body of someone who works out regularly in a gym. His clothes were obviously of high quality, tailored despite their casual appearance, and she couldn't help but be aware of the contrast between his shined shoes and her own bare feet.

She didn't immediately recognize him, but she knew from the smile on his face that he was familiar to her, and obviously her to him. But when he spoke, a jolt of awareness ran through her, knocking her from the spot where she stood.

"Chiara?"

"Ivan! I can't even believe it. What are you doing here?"

She reached up and hugged him warmly, happily surprised.

"I'm in Montreal for my cousin's wedding. I…I couldn't help myself. I hope you don't mind me looking you up?"

"No! Not at all. Come in, come in."

She took in the full sight of his face as she led him into her condo. He was handsome, but not in the youthful way she last remembered him. There were a few distinguished wrinkles around his forehead and eyes, and the thick brown hair he used to boast had been replaced with a closely-shaved buzz to minimize the appearance of his thinning top. He carried himself as someone who was doing well for himself, and Chiara suddenly felt very underdressed.

Pulling out a seat in the kitchen she motioned for him to sit down. "I was working all morning and must have lost track of time. Let me just run and get dressed, then we can catch up." As she left the kitchen her mind was swirling. Having Ivan in her home was surreal and brought back so many memories as well—memories that until now had been sealed in a dusty old box, somewhere on a top shelf in her mind. She found she was curious to know more about his life between then and now, but apprehensive as well.

Her breathing was shallow as she returned to the kitchen and set about making a fresh pot of coffee, then completed the salad she had started before his interruption. True to her upbringing, she didn't ask whether he was hungry or thirsty, but rather assumed he would partake of whatever she put on the table. While keeping her hands busy she asked questions about his life and how he made his living. She learned that he was still residing in Toronto, owning a condo in a downtown skyrise, and after many years in the corporate world now worked as an independent consultant to businesses in the manufacturing industry. She learned that he had been married for seven years but, having experienced the proverbial seven-year itch, had ended the marriage abruptly and without reservation, explaining that "when it isn't right, it isn't right." Finally, they spoke about life in

Toronto, the fast pace, how the city life compared to that of Montreal—Ivan seemed convinced that Chiara would love life in Toronto that much more. By the time they had finished lunch and were enjoying a cup of coffee, Chiara had the full picture of Ivan's life over the past fifteen or so years, and, naturally, couldn't help but compare it to her own.

As if on cue, Ivan finally turned the conversation around. "I'd be lying if I didn't admit that I've kept an eye on you over the years—your career, especially. I'm proud of you, Boop. You've done well."

Boop. The nickname he gave her on their first date, so many years ago, when she had clumsily collided with a waiter carrying a try of drinks. As the waiter staggered, trying to regain balance for both himself and the wobbling tray, Chiara had stood frozen to the ground, only able to utter one single, nonsensical syllable: "Boop." This had stuck with them over the course of their relationship, becoming both a nickname and a term of endearment for Ivan, and for Chiara, a funny memory of the night when she nervously went on their first date. It jarred her to hear it now, the Ivan in her memory colliding with this sleek new Ivan sitting at her kitchen table. She could see from his expression that this was the desired effect.

"You know, I'm also on the Board of Directors for The Art Gallery of Toronto. I have some clout—I could pull some strings." Taken aback, Chiara remained silent. There was something in his tone, in his mannerisms, that she didn't understand, and it was causing her to feel mildly uncomfortable. Ivan mistook her silence as politeness and pushed forward. "It's an international stage, Chiara. You deserve the spotlight."

"Ivan, I—I don't know what to say." Professionally, what he offered was huge. It would take her career to the next level, offering her coveted exposure on the Canadian art scene. It would also ensure her ability to support herself financially for years to come, a factor that had recently taken on renewed importance. It wasn't an offer that she could refuse—that any working artist would refuse—but there was something about the intention in Ivan's eyes that kept her firmly grounded in her seat.

"Say yes, silly. And maybe, if you come to Toronto, we could have dinner... Maybe go for drinks? Reconnect."

Finally, Chiara understood the root of what she was sensing. Transporting back in time to one of their last conversations, where he had assumed she would follow him to Toronto while he completed his master's—and had assumed, in the process, that he knew what was best for her—she had had to make a choice, then, between her heart and her mind. An unnerving wave of déjà vu washed over her and she found herself exhaling from somewhere deep inside her body.

———————

"*Sei stanca*, Chiara?" Nonna sat down on the couch beside Chiara, giving her a gentle rub on the leg. Chiara was resting, her head leaning against the back of the couch, eyes closed.

"*Si*. I am tired, Nonna. Everything is just so...tiring."

"*Capisco*." Continuing on in Italian, her *nonna* began to tell her a story. "You know when your dad was born?"

"Of course, 1944."

"Exactly. In March. And your *nonno* and I got married in October of 1943."

Chiara's eyes were still closed. She generally loved her *nonna*'s stories, she just didn't know if she had the energy for it tonight. Nonetheless, furrowing her brows, she allowed the words to roll around in her mind until they hit the intended target. "Oh! *Oh...*"

"*Si*," her grandmother confirmed.

"Nonna, you rebel."

Nonna laughed and, speaking Italian, continued on with

her story. "I fell in love with your grandfather the year I turned seventeen. I thought he was the most handsome boy I'd ever seen—and he was sweet on me, too. I was a real looker back in my day! Anyway, for months and months we were inseparable, to the point that I couldn't remember life without him in it. But then, he turned eighteen—you know the war was on in the old country, and conscription was mandatory. The night before he joined the army, I had dinner with his family and when he walked me home… *Oops*."

"Oops?"

The old woman shrugged, unashamed.

"Unfortunately, by the time I realized I was pregnant, your *nonno* was at war and I didn't know if or when I would ever see him again. My father was livid, no daughter of his was going to end up with a fatherless child. Times were different, and the mentality back then, especially in a small village like ours—your father would have been labelled a bastard.

"There was another boy in the village, a nice boy. He was a few years older, from a wealthier family, and he'd expressed some interest in me before so, my father decided it was an easy solution. He didn't tell him about the pregnancy but, he pushed for a wedding as quickly as possible. I didn't refuse, but I cried every day. And I prayed for a miracle."

"*Mamma mia*. I can't believe I never knew about any of this!"

"*Boh*. A lady has a right to her secrets."

By this point Chiara was sitting upright, her entire body turned toward the older woman. Her grandmother had always been a woman of great wisdom, but, also, rigid in matters of tradition. She embodied the epitome of the Italian *nonna*, from the short dark curls to the yellow gold cross strung on a chain around her neck. After the death of her husband, Chiara's *nonno*, she had eliminated all colour from her wardrobe, choosing to wear only black, something she considered a respectable symbol of widowhood. Pairing this version of her grandmother with the newest revelations was causing Chiara's head to spin for the second time that day. Her curiosity was undoubtedly peaked, however, and she couldn't help wanting to know more.

"So, what happened?"

"What happened? What do you think happened? The war ended and your grandfather returned."

"You got your miracle."

"*Si.* When it's love, it's love."

Whenever she came to a crossroads, she always found it best to sit deep within herself, to listen for the answer that was always present. Without fail, the answer would always present itself, as long as she was willing to listen.

Picking up the phone, she dialed Ivan's number. He answered immediately.

"Hi, Boop. This is a pleasant surprise."

"Hey, Ivan. You busy?"

"For you, never. Calling to make some travel arrangements?" Ivan sounded confident and self-assured, and it irked Chiara to hear it.

"No...no. The thing is, Ivan—" She paused, debating silently whether her planned approach was still the best approach. Deciding to stay the course, she continued, speaking directly. "Ivan, I couldn't help but feel, earlier, that your offer to help my career came with the assumption that I would date you again."

"Well, Chiara, don't get me wrong here, but you and I *were* always good together. And I *do* have both the ideas and the means to take your career to higher places. That both statements are true is just a happy coincidence."

"In that case, would you be willing to keep things strictly

professional?"

"What do you mean?"

"I mean, you're right, we were good together once upon a time. But that was then, and this is now, and a romantic relationship is not in the cards for us, Ivan. If you meant what you said, that you're willing to put in a good word for me, out of friendship and professional respect—yes, I would be grateful to you for that. But if you didn't—"

"You never did know what was best for you. You're making a mistake, Chiara."

"No, Ivan, I'm not. And I resent that statement. The one thing that hasn't changed between then and now is this assumption you have that you can lead my life better than I can. You keep dangling these carrots before me—come to Toronto, the city is bigger, the galleries are better, your connections are stronger, and you, a real catch of a guy—but I'm not a horse, Ivan. I don't need to be goaded or bribed or enticed. I know what I want, and that isn't it. Now I've done very well for myself so far, and I've led a very good life on my terms and by my rules. I'm not about to change that now, not for you or for anybody else. If you want to help me, we can have a professional discussion about that. But if it was just another carrot, please, keep it for yourself."

Ivan was silent. When he spoke again, his voice was filled with the sound of his own ego. "That's alright, Chiara. You're doing so well on your own, you can just continue on as you are. But, one day in the future, whether it's next week or next month or next year, you will regret this conversation and you'll be tempted to come crawling back. And you know what? I want you to. I want to be able to say 'I told you so,' because you're just a dreamer Chiara, and I live in the real world."

Chiara was not necessarily surprised by Ivan's reaction, but hearing his words brought her a sense of peace. She had confronted him head on, and in doing so had confirmed everything she already knew about the man.

"Goodbye, Ivan. Take care."

CHAPTER TWELVE

The air was damp and cold, the breeze coming off the bay sent a chill up Chiara's spine as she walked down Water Street. She had butterflies in her stomach but was working hard to convince herself that they were due to the exhibition opening that evening.

Paul had set everything up, managing every last detail from her plane ticket to her hotel room. He said that he wasn't leaving anything to chance—by which he meant her, losing her nerve and chickening out altogether—and so was meticulous in his planning. Joanne, the manager of the Cobalt Door Gallery, had told Chiara by phone that she had never worked with an agent as thorough as Paul. Chiara had not bothered to correct Joanne—Paul was not an agent, just a very impassioned friend with the relevant experience.

Stopping to zip up her fall jacket, she caught sight of her reflection in a shop window and paused to consider it. Paul had led the horse to water, alright. She was here, she was in Newfoundland. But she was still undecided on the what or the how or the if that would follow tonight's opening. Her return passage was booked for three days from now—any more, Paul said, and the pressure would be off, giving her time for excuses and delays—therefore she needed to reach a decision, and quickly at that. Her form was still slender, not much had changed there, but the jacket pulled snuggly away from her body, the material taught around her belly. What would Mike think when he saw her? If he saw her? she wondered. She was still attractive, she reasoned, but there were some obvious changes...

Chiara berated herself and continued her walk. After the way she and Mike had parted, she needed to think less about them and their relationship, and more about his right to the information she was here to share with him. It had never been her intention to keep this from him—she knew his history, she knew that she didn't have that right—but she was distraught over all the different possibilities of reactions that went through her mind. *There is only one way to find out how he'll react,* she thought, *but do I have the guts to see this through?* His life was about to be altered forever by someone he'd known for a very short time, and Chiara could think of hundreds of complications to accompany this change, not the least of which was geography. Not for the first time she considered sending a letter by mail or e-mail. Sending a text? Mortified even at herself she shook her head and continued walking.

Focus on short, attainable goals, Chiara. Walk to the hotel. Order some lunch. Take a nap. Go to the gallery. One step at a time. Deal with tomorrow, tomorrow. With renewed determination she lifted her chin, meeting the breeze head on, and pressed on to her destination.

———

Mike pulled his car up in front of the Cobalt Door Gallery and was mildly surprised to find that it did not actually have a cobalt-coloured door, but rather a glass door typical of many storefronts that lined Water Street. He frowned, somehow taking it as a sign that he was doing the wrong thing—or perhaps, looking for an excuse to turn around. Pounding at the steering wheel with his thumb, he waited for a decision to come to him.

Just then the glass door of the gallery opened, and a woman stepped out onto the sidewalk. She was looking directly at him. Taking his cue, he got out of the car.

"Mr. MacCloud?"

"Mike, please. Are you Joanne?"

"Yes, that's right. I was keeping an eye out for you. The opening is in just a few hours, I admit I was getting a little nervous."

Mike eyed the woman, tall and spindly with straight greying hair and colourful glasses. He liked her immediately and felt guilty for causing her any distress. "I apologize, truly. I admit that I don't come to St. John's very often, I think I was procrastinating." This was his second trip to St. John's in four and a half years, both trips being inspired by the woman of the night, by Chiara. He was anxious for many reasons, but his statement had had the desired effect as Joanne laughed and waved off his tardiness.

"Not to worry then. The important thing is that you're here. Would you mind carrying it inside?"

Joanne held the door open as Mike carried his parcel from the back of the car into the gallery. He set it down on the floor, against a wall where a large gap had been reserved especially for him. As he stood his eyes scanned the room, his breath catching as he spun about.

"Wow." Mike was taken aback by the sheer boldness of the display of paintings. He wagered that there were thirty canvases of varying sizes, all of Came to Stay from different angles. The vast majority of paintings were of the beach—whether as breathtaking water views or up-close samples—studies, Joanne called them—of beach items like rocks or algae, but some were from the perspective of one standing on the beach looking inland. All of these shared one aspect with Mike's own painting: his yellow house at the top of the laneway, the highest point before a clear blue sky, giving the viewer's eye a place to rest, followed closely by the house with the green roof next door. It was an impossible observation to ignore. Mike wondered whether he could consider this another olive branch, for that is how he chose to view Chiara's return to Newfoundland—it was an explanation he hoped rang true. His gift to her exhibition, the painting he wholeheartedly believed was deserving of public admiration, was his own olive branch. He hoped, when she saw it that evening, that she would recognize the gesture.

"I want to reiterate how much we appreciate the loan. I promise we will take good care of it and return it to you safe and sound."

"Thank you. I couldn't imagine an exhibition on Came to Stay without including the original painting."

"Do you mind if I ask how the work came into your possession?"

"It was a gift. From the artist."

Joanne nodded, although the expression on her face indicated that she didn't understand why he was being so cloak and dagger with his loan to the gallery, given that the painting was a direct gift from Chiara. Nonetheless, as a professional she sought to reassure Mike. "At your request, the artist has no prior knowledge of your donation. I did, as I'm sure you can understand, have to run it by her agent in Montreal."

"And?"

"Well, he agreed with you, actually." Joanne sounded surprised, even as she said it. "He thinks it will be a valuable addition to the display but, agreed that it would be best to keep it a surprise. I had my doubts initially, given her condition. Will you be coming to the opening tonight? I'm assuming Ms. Costa will be happy to see a familiar face?"

Mike raised an eyebrow at her previous remark but didn't press for details, choosing to respond to her question instead. "Ah. Well. I'm not so sure, really. That is, I haven't quite decided if I will be here this evening. But I wish you all the best on a successful event. Your guests are in for a real treat."

———————

"Ms. Costa! So nice to see you again."

"I'm so sorry I'm late, Joanne. It's so unlike me. I had a nauseous spell before leaving the hotel, I had to let it to pass." Chiara's cheeks flushed, embarrassed by the excuse even if it was true.

"Don't even think about it, I completely understand. I have three of my own and a grandchild on the way, I know all about it." Joanne gave Chiara a wink before directing her into the gallery space. "It's a light crowd so far but the response has been very positive. I anticipate it will thicken once the dinner crowd lets out."

"Oh, that's perfect, Joanne. And thank you again for all the work you've done. Paul was full of praise." They shared a knowing look at the mention of Paul's name, causing Chiara to smile widely before turning toward the room.

Standing there she allowed snippets of conversation to waft over her, as always acknowledging that her life as an artist was dependent on her relationship with the viewer. She couldn't have one without the other. Although it made her vulnerable, it was a part of the process and she gave it due respect.

"…beautiful…"

"…wide brushstrokes…unique style…"

"…feels like home…"

"…this one's not for sale…"

This last bit brought her out of her reverie, and she looked to Joanne before moving deeper into the room. She didn't believe what she was seeing, even as she approached the wall. She found herself reading the tag on the wall in search of meaning or certainty. It read, simply: Title Unknown/On loan from the owner. Chiara whipped around, searching

Joanne's face for an explanation.

"Mr. MacCloud heard about the exhibition from one of the newspaper ads we ran in Bonavista. He contacted me a few weeks ago—Paul thought I should keep it a surprise? Mr. MacCloud made me promise that the painting would be returned, he seems rather attached to it, but I must agree with him that it's a valuable asset to the exhibition. It's quite a stunning piece."

———————

Mike saw Chiara as she approached the gallery on foot. She was wearing a black sweater dress topped with a black blazer, the dark ensemble only accentuating her dark features. Somehow, she looked even more beautiful than ever. His heart caught in his throat for the second time that day, and he knew in an instant that he couldn't stay away. *God, I miss her…*

He was sitting in a coffee shop across from the gallery. He had been sitting here for an hour, arguing with himself. Now, decision made, he exited the café with purpose and strode toward the gallery. There was a table just inside the front entrance and, for lack of anything better to do with his hands, he picked up a loose-leaf paper containing the artist's statement. There was a picture of Chiara at the top, and beside it a quotation: *When I saw you I fell in love. And you smiled because you knew.* Arrigo Boito. To an outsider the quote likely passed as an indication of Chiara's relationship to the environment she had rendered so passionately, but to Mike—another olive branch? He needed to find out.

———————

Chiara spotted Mike first. He looked handsome standing

there by the door—just as tall, just as strong, his waves a little longer but just as thick as ever. Her body reacted to the sight of him, immediately and without warning. It was as though she was back on the beach that day last May, when she first pulled into Came to Stay and met him for the first time. Her body had taken over then as well.

Mike was scanning the room, obviously searching, and stopped short when he spotted her. They stood that way at length, making Joanne uncomfortable as she stood between them. Clearing her throat, she excused herself to see about refreshments.

Mike crossed the room, slowly but assuredly. Chiara could hear the pulsing in her ears with each step. It's only when he was standing in front of her that she allowed herself to breathe.

"You're here. I wasn't expecting you to be here, I wasn't expecting—," she waved her hand about, pointing generally in the direction of the painting. She was at an utter loss for words.

"I am. I couldn't well allow you to come to Newfoundland without saying a hello. And that…Well, that is exactly where it needs to be." He smiled down at her, his eyes so warm it melted her at her core.

"I was going to reach out to you before leaving town. To talk. There are things that we need to discuss. Things I need to tell you—"

"Ms. Costa? Sorry to interrupt. We were wondering if you could answer a few questions for us. When you have a moment, that is." A small group had approached them. The speaker, standing ahead of the rest, was a young man in his twenties, his friends all about the same age. Given her current circumstances Chiara was tempted to tell them to bug off, and still had this thought in mind when Mike interjected.

"It's okay. You're working, I get it. Don't worry about me, I'll stick around."

It was two hours before Chiara could reasonably extract

herself from the crowd. During that time, they contented themselves by stealing glances at each other at any given opportunity. Mike was considerably more at ease since making the decision earlier to cross Water Street, aided now by a glass of wine he'd been grateful to receive. He wondered, momentarily, why her own hands were empty, knowing as he did her proclivity for red wine and seeing, as he saw, how nervous she was in his presence. Chiara had very obviously not been expecting to see him and was visibly jarred by it. Each time she looked at him brought a different expression to her face, sometimes excited, sometimes anxious, sometimes happy, sometimes fearful.

She needed to speak with him, she knew that was the only way to settle her nerves. Finishing up a small speech before the crowd where she thanked the Cobalt Door and Joanne— as well as her rock, and bulldog of an 'agent' Paul—for all their efforts in hosting an exhibition so dear to her heart, she quietly took her leave. She approached Mike with apprehension but, was carrying both their jackets. "Would you mind walking me back to the hotel? I have things I need to say."

They walked in relative silence, Mike waiting for Chiara to speak and, Chiara waiting for the words to come. They didn't come easily, and by the time they arrived at the hotel she had no choice but to invite him up to her room.

Slipping out of her shoes and into a pair of fuzzy slippers, her feet immediately relieved, she poured two glasses of water and summoned the courage to speak.

"What happened to you that day? You just…left."

Mike, sitting on a chair by the window, accepted the water with a nod. "You left too. I came home and you were just *gone*."

"I *had* to leave, though. I didn't have a choice. But you— one minute we're having a wonderful time, the next, *poof*."

Mike sighed. "You're right. You're absolutely right. And I've kicked myself every day ever since." He bent forward, placing his elbows on his knees, and continued, thoughtfully. "You mentioned that morning, about how your trip was almost over and you'd be returning home, and I panicked. I loved a woman and lost her once in my life, Chiara. I didn't want to go through it again. And I thought, even if you extended your trip it was only delaying the inevitable. You would leave me. Simply put, I panicked."

At another time, and with a different man, Chiara might have lost interest by this point. The mere idea of someone panicking over whether or not to spend more time with her would have caused past-Chiara to roll her eyes and turn away, claiming that she didn't have time in her busy life for such nonsense. But this was Mike—*her* Mike—and he'd said something she could hardly ignore. "What did you mean by 'you didn't want to go through that again'?"

He sat up then, looking at her intensely. She found herself swimming in his blue eyes, the same way she had so many months ago. "Chiara, you have to know how I feel about you, especially after those days we spent together. Chiara—I loved you from the start." She dropped to the bed, feeling a rush of joy that she hadn't experienced since their last day together in May. Mike continued. "I know I shouldn't have just taken off like that, that was wrong of me. After leaving you, I came here to St. John's. To the cemetery." She looked up but, didn't say anything. "I realized that I loved you, but I had all these other emotions mixed in. Guilt being one of them. And I had this urgent need to get it all out in the open, to confess to my family—strange as that may sound—to get their blessing, and also to get closure. I wanted to start with a clean slate with you so, it was just something I needed to do."

"Oh, Mike. I wish I had known."

"When I got back and you weren't there—Why weren't you there? What did you mean when you said you *had* to leave?"

It was Chiara's turn to bow her head forward, heavy as

her body was with the plethora of sudden emotion. "I got a call from my mom shortly after you left. My dad was sick. Very sick. I rebooked my flight as soon as I could and left. By that point I wasn't thinking of anything other than getting home to him. As it was, I didn't have very much time with him before he…before he died."

Whether it was the shock of seeing Mike, hearing him express his love for her, the memory of discovering her dad's illness and that last, frantic day in Came to Stay, or the pregnancy hormones making her feel everything with heightened intensity, much without warming she began to cry. She cried deep, heaving, painful tears. She cried for the lost time with her dad, the time she lost with Mike; she cried for the secret her dad had kept from her, for the choice she had been denied in his last few weeks; she cried for the miscommunication with Mike and the grief it had caused them both, and for the joy she felt at this renewed opportunity. She cried on behalf of her mom and *nonna*, and she cried the tears she hadn't cried while being strong for them. And finally, she cried on behalf of the newest generation, months away from being mixed into the fold. She cried because she didn't yet know what the future held for this little one, but, as she cried, she came to understand that everything would be alright.

Mike had come to her, sitting beside her and holding her through the tears. He stroked her hair, her back, kissing her on the head and cheek, by reflex wanting to kiss the pain away. As the tears subsided, he could feel a calm come over her body as he held her in his arms.

She was ready to tell him the one thing she was most afraid to say.

"I'm pregnant."

"I know."

"It's yours."

"I know."

"It'll be okay."

He smiled. Guiding her chin upward he kissed her deeply and firmly, erasing any doubts in the process. "I know."

"Mike?"

"Yeah?"

"I love you."

CHAPTER THIRTEEN

Mike pulled the car off the laneway and into the driveway. Chiara was so excited that she jumped from the car as soon as it was in park, bounding up the steps even before the engine was cut.

"Wow. Mike! It's amazing!"

He smiled widely as he exited the car, partly because of how happy it made him to be home, especially on a crisp May day such as this one, but mostly because he wasn't returning home alone. He gave her his most boyishly crooked grin. "You like?"

"I love."

The new porch was easily triple the size of the original porch, spanning the entire width of the house, and stretching several feet in length. The porch continued around the northern corner of the house, allowing for a full panorama of the ocean and shoreline. The view was breathtaking. Chiara could imagine sipping her morning coffee while sitting on an Adirondack chair before this view or, taking their evening meals on a patio set from the far corner, watching the sunsets together as they did the previous May.

As though reading her mind Mike spoke as he came up the steps. "We can get some furniture for it this summer. I really didn't use it much last year once it was built. I guess I didn't see the point, really." Setting the baby's bucket seat down on the solid floor, his eyes went soft at the sight of his daughter sleeping soundly from the long drive. "Something tells me this porch will see much more activity this summer."

Chiara walked over, wrapping her arms around Mike's waist. Mike put an arm around her in turn, pulling her closer to him, liking the feel of her against him. Together they watched the tiny face. The baby's mouth puckered, then parted, the tiny lips opening and closing in her sleep as though she was rooting. Chiara's breasts began to tingle at the sight. The baby would wake up hungry soon.

"It amazes me still, you know, that I'm a mom now. Some women get to forty and their kids are all grown up, teenagers getting ready to leave the nest. Here I am just starting out. But I don't think I could have done it any differently, I wasn't ready at twenty-five or thirty, or even thirty-five. Now, now I feel like I can give all my attention to motherhood without any distractions. I couldn't have done that before. And looking at her sweet face, I *want* to give her my full attention, I don't care about anything else."

"You would have made a great mom no matter what and no matter when. I know it. I see you with her. You *are* a great mom."

Chiara wasn't convinced that what Mike said was true. All those years spent with a singular focus on her career required a certain amount of self-imposed selfishness. She had needed all her energy and all her concentration in order to accomplish all that she had accomplished professionally. Had she been a mother sooner, perhaps her career would still have taken off, but perhaps it would never have left the ground; perhaps she would have found a successful balance, or perhaps she would have grown resentful over a lost dream. She would never know, obviously, but, standing there with her arms around her man and her baby in sight—finally, a tribe of her own—she was reminded of another one of her *nonna*'s favourite expressions: Everything happens at the perfect time. Not sooner, not later. And nothing was more perfect to Chiara than this precise moment.

With a full heart, she gave Mike a tight squeeze. "Well, it definitely helps to have her great dad by my side. Might have been physically possible to have kids before now but, there has never been another you."

"Ha! Thank goodness for that!"

She elbowed him in the ribs, playfully. "I'm being serious, Mike MacCloud. My life would never have been the same had I not met you."

He turned and wrapped his second arm around her also, pulling her into a great bear hug, pressing his face deep into her hair. "Thank goodness for that." This time his tone was sincere and full of emotion.

Chiara had returned to Montreal, alone, after the opening of the exhibition. Her OB-GYN was there, and her prenatal care was already well underway by the time Mike and Chiara reconnected in St. John's. Plus, she knew that she couldn't deprive her mother of her one and only opportunity to experience becoming a *nonna* in her own right. Her mom and *nonna* had grasped on to the news of Chiara's pregnancy with all hands, making her their centre of attention the way only, she felt, an Italian mother can. Her mom would call her daily to ask how she was feeling and, would insist that Chiara go over for supper at least once per week so she could ensure, with her own eyes, that Chiara was eating enough. Even after the baby was born, Chiara would still find pots of soup or casserole dishes of ready-to-bake lasagna left by her front door. The attention could be a bit much by times, but Chiara also recognized that the gift of a new life had lifted the women out of their grief as much as it had lifted her out of hers.

Mike had stayed behind to winterize the house and take care of a few practicalities. He made plans with Bill and Cheryl regarding mail and general maintenance, and hashed out a plan with Finn over what each man would need to cover

over the winter months.

After meeting with Ted and Ron that day in June, Mike had left understanding two things. First, he was very much inspired by the prospect of a new business. After years of hibernation he needed a project he could sink his teeth into. However, as much as he respected Ted, something hadn't been right about that particular prospect. Sitting with Finn at a pub in Trinity—the same pub where he and Chiara had celebrated her birthday—he had laid his cards out on the table. Luckily, Finn was in agreement and together, they hashed out a business model for an ecotourism company that each man could get behind. Aside from Chiara, or, perhaps, because of her, it was the only thing that caused the blood to rush through his veins since leaving his previous career. In the months between losing Chiara and finding her again, he had poured all his energy into the new business so that, by the time Mike and Chiara had their heart-to-heart last October, he had already invested a significant amount of money and time into the business he and Finn were building. Given that it had been his brainchild, it wouldn't have been right to abandon Finn during their inaugural season.

When he discussed his new business venture with Chiara, it was her that that had suggested they return to Came to Stay after the baby's birth—and after the worst of the winter was over, she specified. Spending an entire spring and summer searching for beach treasures with her daughter in tow sounded like a small piece of heaven to her, and she knew it would relieve some of Mike's anxiety also, to have them with him.

It had taken a matter of weeks, all told, before Mike was able to join Chiara in Montreal. It was the first time he had ever left Newfoundland, and he was inundated with a lifetime's worth of new experiences within a matter of months. He found the city to be loud and vibrant, and although he wasn't used to hearing such an array of language over the course of a given day, he got used to the melodic rhythm of the French language and grew to enjoy circumstances where he could hear both English and French being spoken interchangeably. He also wasn't used to the array of food that was available to him in Montreal, and he and Chiara made a point of dining at a new restaurant every week just so he could take in the sheer vastness of different cuisines—giving them, also, an opportunity to maximize on their time together before adding a baby to the relationship. Chiara felt like she was discovering her city anew through Mike's eyes. As someone who had lived alone her entire adult life, she was surprised to find how thoroughly she was enjoying Mike's company and how easily he had integrated into her life. As two islands, come together, they had a remarkable ability to exist in harmony.

The months had passed in this way, facing each first and milestone together. They spent Mike's birthday at a cabin in the Quebec woods, their first Christmas with Chiara's family—or, Mike's new Italian family, as they liked to refer to themselves—and they spent a quiet New Year's Eve celebrating alone together in the cozy warmth of Chiara's condo.

Chiara's due date was, perhaps ironically, Valentine's Day—something she wasn't thrilled about, her inner sense of pragmatism beating out her inner romantic. In truth, it was simply too corny for her to bear. However, her contractions began a few days ahead of schedule, and by five in the morning on Friday, February 13th, Stella Maya MacCloud was born.

"Poor wee thing," Mike had said through his tears. "Being born on Friday the 13th, she'll never live that down."

"It's okay," Chiara had assured him. "She has Italian genes after all. Thirteen is a lucky number for us, it's like winning the jackpot."

"Indeed," was Mike's only response as he kissed first the top of Stella's head, then the top of Chiara's.

And now they were back in Newfoundland, back in Came

to Stay, back to the stars and water after which their child had been named.

Chiara loosened her arms around Mike's waist and, looking up into the intense blue eyes their daughter now shared, gave herself over to the feeling of complete contentment she now felt. Mike leaned down and kissed her softly on the lips, returning the feeling.

From across the driveway they heard a door open, then shut. "Well, I'll be... I thought I heard a car pull up." Bill reopened the door to the house and called in. "Cheryl! Come on out! Ye'll want to see this!" The door closed and opened a few more times before they heard a high-pitched squeal as Cheryl clapped her hands together.

"Would you look at what the cat dragged in. We've missed ya around here, b'y."

Mike gave a hearty laugh and waved Bill and Cheryl over. "Come on over, there're some people here I'd love for you to meet."

And so it was that a few minutes later, pleasantries over, the four adults were standing in a semi-circle, staring down at the sleeping babe—the Boyds with the air of grandparents preparing for many summers of hugs and treats with the little one, and Chiara and Mike, boasting from the opportunity to show off their new offspring—that Stella finally awoke from her lengthy nap. She looked up at the smiling faces with questioning eyes, before scrunching up her own face, then, grunting loudly, pushing out the gas that had built in her sleeping belly. Her face immediately relaxed, and as she looked up again at the group of adults, she broke out into wide, crooked smile as she settled her blue eyes on her mother's face.

"That's my girl," Chiara grinned.

The Boyds nodded their heads at once, Bill letting out a hoot, and Cheryl a chuckle. "Yes, b'y. There she blows!"

But it was Mike, after looking around the group before settling his laughing eyes back on his daughter, who had the last word.

"Some proud. Some proud, indeed."

EPILOGUE

"What about Toronto and Vancouver?"

"Still in the works, I just asked that the dates be pushed back by a few months. We're splitting our time between Montreal and Newfoundland, at least for now, so fall and winter are the best times for me to arrange exhibits and meetings with curators. Luckily the Came to Stay show has taken on a life of its own, but I'll use my summers to gather new inspiration. Besides, for the moment I'm still on maternity leave."

"And how is the little gummy bear? How is motherhood?"

"Everything I imagined it to be, and everything I didn't know it could be. To think how determined I was to avoid it for so long, and now it's just so...so natural. Like being a mom is what I was always meant to be. I have a hard time imagining life other than how it currently is." Chiara looked over at the floor where Mike was sitting, cross-legged, changing their daughter's diaper. He was making facial expressions and speaking gibberish as he went, resulting in squeals of joy from the little one. The sight brought a surge of warmth to her heart and she added, "I am beginning to learn that it is actually possible to possess multiple passions, and to have many forms of love in one life. I was compartmentalizing between personal and professional, but I see, now, that one does not necessarily detract from another. Changes it, surely. But for better? For worse? I think, maybe, these are just words. In the end it all comes down to choices. Now, at this point in my life, this is my choice."

Paul let out an understanding *hmm* from the other end of the line. "So, is this the point where you thank me?" Paul was chuckling to himself, having meant it sarcastically, and didn't immediately realize that the tone on the other end had turned serious. Finally noticing the silence, he paused. "Chiara?"

"It's true, you know. I do have much to thank you for."

"Oh, go on." He was dismissing her, but she would have none of it.

"No, I'm being serious. If it weren't for you, I would never have found Came to Stay—would never have known it even existed. I would never have come here, would never have met Mike. I would not have had any of this. I would probably still be binge-watching shows over a bottle of wine every night, too."

"Oh, come now. I know you. You would never have allowed yourself to wallow for that long."

"Maybe not. But, still, this…" Her voice trailed off. She couldn't define all that 'this' meant, it was more than words could measure. But Paul had been her catalyst, and she would forever be grateful.

"I told you that I would lead the horse to water, right? But that's where my role ended. You did the rest yourself. Don't ever forget that."

"I won't, Paul. Trust me, I won't."

There was an unexpected knock at the door as she was saying her goodbyes with Paul, and Chiara turned to Mike with a questioning glance. He shrugged as he got up from the floor. It was Bill, wearing work clothes and an old cap on his head.

"Hallo, Mike. I was just wonderin' if ye were available to give me hand? I need to carry the kitchen table out front. The missus wants it repainted, but she can't much handle the smell of paint in the house."

Mike peaked around the back of the door, meeting Chiara's eye. She began to laugh, then choke and cough, dropping to the floor on her back, unable to suppress herself.

"Something wrong with the lady?"

Mike turned back around to Bill, his cheeks slightly flushed but, he hoped, not enough for Bill to notice. "Nah, not at all. Just the baby making her laugh. Not a problem, Bill, I'll come straight away."

He and Chiara exchanged one last look before he grabbed his shoes and headed outdoors. Try as he might, he couldn't wipe the smile from his face.

REFERENCES

The excerpt found in Chapter Five is taken from the book *Klee Wyck* by artist Emily Carr, published in 1941.

The opening quotation is from *Hundreds and Thousands: The Journals of Emily Carr*, published in 1966.

CPSIA information can be obtained
at www.ICGtesting.com
Printed in the USA
LVHW081045021220
673131LV00045B/777

9 781716 048180